AMELIA & ME

BOOK 1 *of the*
GINNY ROSS Series

—◆—

HEATHER STEMP

NIMBUS
PUBLISHING
— NIMBUS.CA —

PRAISE FOR AMELIA & ME

Shortlisted for the 2014–15 Red Cedar Award

"The historical details, the architecture of the town, the daily cuisine (toast with blueberry jam, baked cod and winter vegetables), the currency in pounds, the encounter with a young union organizer named Smallwood on the passenger train, all make for a rich, solid background. And Ginny makes a great protagonist, full of grit. She brings gumption and momentum to the narrative."
—**St. John's** *Telegram*

"Stemp's frank and unsentimental portraits of hardship and forbearance ring especially true. It would be hard for them not to, as Stemp has based the town and characters on her own life. And there are photos to prove it!

This novel for young adults had this not-so-young adult reader captivated with the landscape of Newfoundland, the history of aviation and travel, and the characters of Ginny and her friends from beginning to end."
—**Edwards Book Club**

"[*Amelia and Me*] is appealing because of the historical and regional setting (Great Depression in Newfoundland), the photos of some of the principal characters and locations, and the colourful cast of characters, including the iconic aviator, Amelia Earhart."
—**Canadian Review of Materials**

"[Stemp's] description of life in Harbour Grace in the 1930s rings true in every detail. Her protagonist is charming, warts and all, and we are inspired by her stubborn determination to fly in our dreams."
—**Resource Links**

"Based on the girlhood experiences of the author's aunt, this charming historical novel gives girls a spirited and likeable heroine."
—**Canadian Children's Book News**

Nimbus Publishing Limited
3660 Strawberry Hill St, Halifax, NS, B3K 5A9
(902) 455-4286 nimbus.ca

Printed and bound in Canada
NB1504

This story is a work of fiction, inspired by a true story.

Originally published in 2013 by Pennywell Books (Flanker Press)

Cover and interior design: Heather Bryan

Library and Archives Canada Cataloguing in Publication

Title: Amelia & me / Heather Stemp.
Other titles: Amelia and me
Names: Stemp, Heather, 1945- author.
Description: Series statement: Ginny Ross series ; book 1
 Previously published: St. John's, Newfoundland and Labrador:
 Pennywell Books Ltd, ©2013.
Identifiers: Canadiana (print) 2020015916X
 Canadiana (ebook) 20200159178 | ISBN 9781771088244 (softcover)
 ISBN 9781771088251 (HTML)
Subjects: LCSH: Earhart, Amelia, 1897-1937—Juvenile fiction.
Classification: LCC PS8637.T46 A64 2020 | DDC jC813/.6—dc23

Nimbus Publishing acknowledges the financial support for its publishing activities from the Government of Canada, the Canada Council for the Arts, and from the Province of Nova Scotia. We are pleased to work in partnership with the Province of Nova Scotia to develop and promote our creative industries for the benefit of all Nova Scotians.

This book is for Ginny's great-great-nephews and nieces:
Caleb, Maeve, Charles, and Phaedra

A LL OF THE main characters in this story are real people. Ginny was my aunt, her mom and dad were my grandparents, and her brother, Billy, was my father. Aunt Rose was my great-aunt and Uncle Harry was my great-uncle. Since this is historical fiction, you can look up unfamiliar terms in the glossary, which begins on page 221.

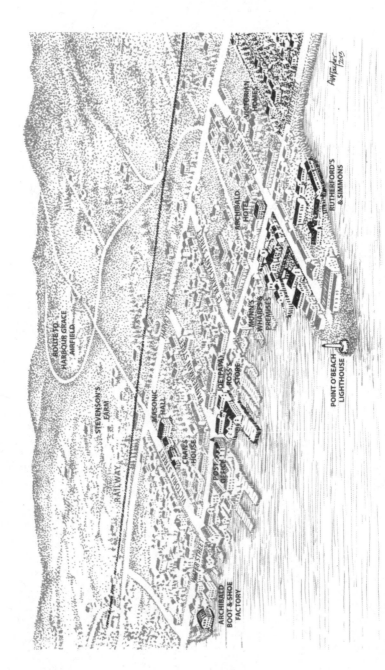

Adapted from a map of Harbour Grace, 1879, engraver and publisher unknown.

CONTENTS

PART ONE

PART TWO

PART ONE

CHAPTER ONE

AUGUST 1931

⊷◇⊶

E VEN IN AUGUST the early morning in Newfoundland was
cold. I snuggled under my quilt until the grandfather
clock in the parlour struck three. Then I swung my legs
over the side of the bed and reached into the warmth under
the covers for my clothes. I wiggled out of my nightgown
and quickly pulled on my navy dress and red sweater. With
my lucky penny wrapped in a hanky and tucked into my
pocket, I grabbed my socks and shoes.

The third-floor hallway was quiet as I tiptoed past Mom's
bedroom door and the messy hole my brother called his
bedroom. The stairs creaked. But if I stuck to the banister
side, I should be safe. Still, with every step, I imagined
Mom's voice shouting down to me, "Ginny Ross, you get
back here!"

On the second floor the only sound was the distant
rumble of my grandfather's snoring in the bedroom at the
end of the hall. Nana said it was a miracle she got any sleep

with the racket Papa made. I turned and headed down the inside stairs to the store.

On the bottom step I pulled on my socks and shoes. A dozen giant steps to the front door and I slid the steel bolt to one side. That was when my plan fell apart. If I left through the front door, then I wouldn't be able to lock it behind me. At 7:00 A.M., when Papa came down to open up, he'd know someone had gone out.

I quickly scanned the store. The front windows on either side of the door didn't open—no escape route there. Behind the counters, floor-to-ceiling shelves piled with groceries lined the side walls. The four windows on the back wall overlooked the bay, but opening them wouldn't help. The drop to the ground was at least twelve feet because the basement led out to the backyard.

That was it! The basement.

The trap door at the end of the short counter was hidden by a box of carrots. I pushed it out of the way and pulled up the door by its rope handle. A damp, earthy smell greeted me at the top of the ladder. I took a deep breath and climbed down the first two rungs. They groaned under my weight, but I couldn't turn back. I was already late.

I grabbed the rope on the underside of the trap door, eased it back into place, and felt my way down to the dirt floor. In the darkness I turned and stretched my arms out in front of me. By the time I found a path through the crates and barrels, my elbows and knees were some sore. I got to the basement door and tugged it open. A cold wind off the bay hit my face.

The moon and stars shone brightly, so I stayed in the shadows close to the stone walls of the store. Voices came from down by the wharf, but there was no one in sight. I crossed Water Street, slipped into the darkness beside Strapp's Pharmacy, and then cut through their back garden to avoid the street light at the corner of Victoria. When I emerged farther up the hill, my cousin Pat Cron stood in front of her house, waving at me to hurry.

The uphill climb tired me out, but I had to keep moving. Halfway up I bent over to catch my breath. When I straightened up and tried to run, I could barely lift my knees. My chest hurt and I panted like an old dog on a hot summer day. Finally I joined Pat, who pulled me into the shadow of the nearest house.

She turned and whispered in my face. "You'd be a better runner if you lost a few pounds."

"And you'd still be in bed if I hadn't told you about my plan."

Pat smiled. "You've got me there." She took my hand and pulled me toward Stevenson's farm, which lay beyond the top end of Victoria Street. As I trotted along beside her, she occasionally gave my arm a tug to remind me I was moving too slowly.

I raised my head to see how much farther we had to climb and saw Jennie Mae Stevenson running down to meet us. Her dad's breakfast pail swung in her hand. Mr. Stevenson ran their farm and also worked part-time as the night watchman for the Harbour Grace Airport Trust. It was his job to keep people away from the planes. If he caught us, Jennie Mae would say we were just bringing his breakfast.

She stopped in front of Pat and me, and the pail stopped swinging. "I've been thinking about your plan, and there's something we haven't considered," she said. "If we get caught by someone other than my dad, he could lose his job."

"So we won't get caught," Pat replied. She stepped around Jennie Mae and carried on up the hill.

"She couldn't care less about what happens to my dad," Jennie Mae whispered to me. "To her we're just those people from up the hill."

I took her hand and we continued walking. "Has she ever said that to you?" I asked.

"A few times," she replied. "But not when you're around. She's usually with Alice Brant."

Since Pat was my cousin, our parents expected us to do everything together. Usually that was fine with me because Pat could be a lot of fun. But she'd changed. She was moody and unpredictable. Instead of hanging around with Jennie Mae, me, and the rest of the grade sevens, she preferred to be with Alice Brant and her gang of grade eights.

Alice was a snob. Her father owned the biggest fishing fleet in Harbour Grace, and she thought she was right special. In fact, that was how Jennie Mae and I became friends: I stood up to Alice when she called Jennie Mae a farmer's brat.

I glanced over at her. Her worried frown prompted me to stop and raise my right hand. "I promise I'll be careful, and between the two of us, we'll keep Pat under control."

She sighed. "I suppose that's all we can do at this point." Pat was way ahead; she waved at us to hurry. I took Jennie Mae's hand again and we continued our uphill climb. In less than five minutes, we crossed the railroad track and joined Pat at the Stevensons' farm.

"Come on, you two." She grabbed my other hand and dragged Jennie Mae and me behind her. "You're as slow as molasses in January."

I didn't bother answering because I knew she would comment on my weight again.

A left turn and we climbed to the height of land that formed the airstrip. First we saw the light in the window of Mr. Stevenson's shack. Then, there it was: the City of New York—the most beautiful plane I'd ever seen. It was only a silhouette against the early morning sky, but I knew its colours. It was painted maroon, with cream-coloured wings and cream letters down the fuselage to tell us its name.

A rectangle of light shone into the night. Mr. Stevenson had opened his door. We scurried onto the rocks on the south side of the airstrip. We crouched down and pulled our dresses over our legs to keep warm while he inspected the plane.

We'd been some excited when the plane landed yesterday afternoon. This was the last flight until next summer, so a huge crowd came out. Even when the City of New York was no more than a speck in the sky, we all cheered. It touched down, taxied to the end of the runway near the watchman's shack, turned around, and stopped. And there it sat, still surrounded by the rope fence tied to empty oil barrels to keep everyone away.

We knew from the story in the *Harbour Grace Standard* who to expect. Mr. Brown, the pilot, emerged through the hatch above the cockpit. When Mr. Mears, the owner of the plane, climbed out of the side door, everyone cheered louder. He held a fluffy white dog, who barked at the crowd.

The newspaper went on to say the three of them would take off at 7:00 A.M. to fly around the world. But I knew a secret about the flight. I heard Uncle Harry talking to Papa in the store last night. Uncle Harry was the airport supervisor. He said Mr. Mears and Mr. Brown were not taking off at 7:00 A.M. Instead, they were leaving before dawn.

I barely had time to go to Jennie Mae's house and then to Pat's to tell them the news before Mom sent me off to bed. A lot of people were going to be disappointed, but not the three of us.

CHAPTER TWO

IMPULSE

———◄○►———

P AT, JENNIE MAE, and I watched the light from Mr. Stevenson's lantern as he walked back into the watchman's shack. We waited a few more minutes to be on the safe side before crawling over the rocks onto the edge of the runway. The wind whipped my hair and I had to hold down the bottom of my dress. I pulled the other two close to me and whispered, "Are you ready?"

They both nodded. Pat led our run to the plane.

We stopped in the shadow of the wing and listened to the wind whistling in the struts. I reached up and placed my hands on the fuselage. The wood siding was cold and the nails felt even colder. With one finger I traced the C in the word City.

Jennie Mae put the handle of the breakfast pail over her arm, and she and Pat reached up too. With each gust of wind I felt the plane trembling. To calm it, I ran my hands along one side. "Hello, City of New York," I whispered. "Welcome to Harbour Grace, Newfoundland."

Pat and Jennie Mae followed me around the tail, along the opposite side, and back along the fuselage to the side door. We were safer there, with the plane between us and the shack. I whispered, "On this night—"

"The City of New York will be the ninth plane to fly across the Atlantic from Harbour Grace," Pat butted in.

"Forget the news report," Jennie Mae whispered. "We have to go before my dad gets into trouble." She grabbed our hands and pulled us away from the plane.

"Relax, will you?" Pat tried to pull her hand away.

"Not until I get you into my dad's shack," Jennie Mae replied.

"What about my plan?" I whispered.

Jennie Mae dropped my hand. "I forgot," she said. "Just hurry."

I turned toward the plane.

"Hey, I'm staying, too," Pat said.

I glanced over my shoulder. Pat was trying to jerk free, but Jennie Mae was holding on. I ran back to the plane, placed my hands on the door, and whispered my good-luck charm as fast as I could. "On this night of dark and light, trust me friend to see you right. Remember me in wind and rain, and I will bring you home again."

"Let me go," Pat shouted into Jennie Mae's face.

"Who's out there?" It was Mr. Stevenson's voice.

I ducked under the fuselage and peeked over the wheel cover.

"It's just me, Dad," Jennie Mae shouted.

"Who else is there?" Mr. Stevenson asked.

"Uh.…" Jennie Mae glanced in my direction. "Just Pat Cron and me."

"You two get over here right now!"

Jennie Mae released Pat's arm and she jerked it away.

"Farmer's brat," Pat said with disgust.

I sat down behind the wheel cover and waited until their voices died away. Then I crawled out and placed my hands on the fuselage again. For as long as I could remember, I had loved planes. But I'd never seen the inside of one.

Slowly I stepped up on the wheel cover and grasped the door handle, just to look in. When I pulled myself up, the handle turned in my hand and the door swung open like an invitation.

I reached inside the plane and my hands touched a bundle of wires running along the floor. By hanging on to them, I wriggled forward on my stomach. I lifted one leg in and then the other. I scrambled around on all fours and peeked outside before I gently closed the door.

CHAPTER THREE

FLIGHT

———◄○►———

THE INSIDE OF the plane was dark and quiet. I sat back on my heels and peered out the window. There was no one around. Except for the odd gust of wind buffeting the plane, all was silent.

I looked around my small space. Aside from a leather seat with a high back, this part of the plane was completely filled by a huge tank. Uncle Harry said the City of New York carried 450 gallons of extra fuel to get across the Atlantic Ocean. My nose told me this was it.

Over the tank the cockpit was visible. But how could I get there? Mr. Brown used the hatch over the pilot's seat, but I could never climb the outside of the plane the way he did. Not only that, Mr. Stevenson would see me way up there.

I thought for a few seconds and then took a very deep breath. By making myself as skinny as possible, I squeezed between the tank and the side wall. Baby steps moved me to the front of the plane where another small space led to the cockpit door. I felt like Alice bending down to pass through one of the doors in Wonderland. And what I saw truly was wondrous!

I slipped into the pilot's seat and ran my hands over the softness of the leather. Then I gently touched the switches and dials on the instrument board. They looked like the ones in Aunt Rose's Model T Ford, but there were so many more. I ran my fingers over each instrument and wondered which ones Mr. Brown checked after he started the engine.

Through the windshield the only thing I saw was the early morning sky. The stars were gone, but the moon still shone. Thanks to Uncle Harry I knew a lot about the planes that landed and took off from Harbour Grace. This one, a Lockheed Vega, was a tail dragger. Until the tail lifted on takeoff, and the plane was more level, the view was very limited.

I hesitated for a few seconds before I grasped the throttle and closed my eyes. I imagined the rope fence dropping and the chocks in front of the wheels sliding away. I felt my plane trembling with anticipation. I started the engine and pushed the throttle forward. Faster and faster I rolled down the runway until I soared up over the trees, banked left, and headed toward the bay.

"Off we go into the wild blue yonder," I sang over the roar of the engines. All of Harbour Grace stretched out below me like a giant Christmas tree, yellow street lights looping up the hillside.

Along Water Street I looked for familiar landmarks. The clock tower on the post office was higher than any other roof or chimney, and there was Papa's store right next door. The white printing on the side wall said *Joseph Ross Household Goods and Ships Provisions.*

Farther down Water Street I flew over the huge warehouses, sheds, and wharves at Rutherford's, Simmons's, and Munn's, where the fishermen prepared their boats for the morning catch. Beyond the business section Victorian houses with long front gardens and views of the bay stood dark and quiet. Their owners didn't have to be at work for many hours.

I banked left at Bear's Cove and headed back to town. Over the houses where my friends still slept in their warm beds, I skimmed the roofs and waved. I moved faster than everyone—no more panting up hills, no more bending over to catch my breath, and no more "molasses in January."

Then I heard a car door slam.

Suddenly, I was back in the real world.

I looked out the small side window next to the pilot's seat. Over toward the rocky ridge, a car had arrived. A man was getting out, and then another one. And now there was a third man. It was Uncle Harry. Mr. Stevenson joined them. They made their way toward the plane—all four of them. It was too late to get out!

I crouched in the small space between the door leading to the cockpit and the gas tank. My heart pounded so hard

I was afraid it would burst. The crunch of footsteps on the gravel got closer and closer. With my back against the side of the plane, I hugged my knees to make myself smaller. The voices were right outside.

"I'll leave you gentlemen to discuss the flight," Mr. Stevenson said. "You know where to find me if you need anything."

"Thanks, John." It was Uncle Harry's voice. No one else spoke until Mr. Stevenson walked away.

"Are you ready to listen to reason, Henry?"

"I want this speed record, George."

It was Henry Mears, the owner of the plane, and George Brown, his pilot.

"Feel the wind as you're standing here," Uncle Harry said. "You're partially protected by this rocky ridge. When you get to the end of it, you have Lady Lake on your right and the bay on your left. A stronger wind could gust from either side. Stick to your original plan and leave at seven."

Mr. Mears didn't reply.

"At least walk down to where the ridge ends and feel the wind for yourself," Mr. Brown said.

There was a pause, and the plane door opened. Something thumped onto the floor and the door slammed shut. A scratching sound, from the opposite side of the gas tank. My heart pounded again. The seconds ticked by.

Then a furry white face poked around the tank. It was Mr. Mears's dog! I had forgotten all about him. He ran into the cockpit and jumped up on the pilot's seat. For a few seconds neither of us moved. Then he poked his face around the seat and sniffed the air. I was afraid to breathe. He looked over, saw me, and started yapping.

"Quiet, Tailwind," Mr. Mears yelled back to the plane.

Tailwind crouched down and growled.

"Nice doggy," I whispered.

He barked again.

"Shhh! Mr. Stevenson will lose his job," I whispered. "Not to mention what will happen to me."

He barked louder.

"Tailwind, that's enough," Mr. Mears shouted from farther down the runway.

That's all I needed—someone coming back to shut up the dog. I wiped my forehead with the back of my hand. There was nowhere to hide. I had to get out, but I was afraid the men were still too close to the plane.

I waited another few minutes. The growling was softer now. I stood up and peeked over the pilot's seat to look out the windshield. Tailwind looked up at me and moved to the farthest corner of the cockpit. I smiled at him and wiped my forehead again. Now that I was taller than him, he was much quieter. I just hoped he would stay that way.

Down the runway the men approached the end of the rocky ridge. I could see the three of them, but not clearly. From the side window next to the pilot's seat, this end of the ridge appeared to be about thirty feet from the plane. With a little luck I could be in the rocks before they noticed me.

I squeezed my way back to Mr. Mears's seat. Then I heard a familiar scratching sound from the opposite side of the gas tank. Tailwind was following me. I couldn't let him get out. A quick turn of the door handle and I jumped. My right knee smashed against something and I let out a gasp. I must have hit the back edge of the wheel cover.

When I rolled over, Tailwind appeared in the opened door. I stood up to close it and a shooting pain made me bite my lip. Now that I was out of his plane, he wagged his tail and smiled down at me. On another day I'd probably have smiled back, but not that day. I gently pushed him back and closed the door.

My right leg wouldn't hold my weight, so I ended up doing a step-drag, step-drag across the runway. I was halfway to the ridge when someone called out.

"Hey, you!"

CHAPTER FOUR

ESCAPE

I TURNED TOWARD the voice from down the runway and saw Mr. Mears, Mr. Brown, and Uncle Harry in the distance. One of them started running toward me. It looked like Mr. Mears.

"Stop!" he yelled.

My step-drag sped up. When I reached the ridge, I squeezed through the first few big rocks and pushed myself into a deep crevice in the boulders behind. I was shaking so hard, I was sure he would hear my teeth chattering.

"You better come out of there right now!" The voice was gruff. It sounded like Mr. Mears and he must have been out of shape. He sure was panting a lot.

I pushed myself farther back and held the bottom of my dress tightly around my legs.

"Do you hear me?"

It was Mr. Mears. I saw him through a chink in the rocks and he was coming awfully close. I held my breath.

He scanned the rock face. A minute or two passed, but it seemed like an hour.

"It's four thirty, Henry," Mr. Brown shouted across the runway. "If you insist on getting off the ground before sunrise, we've only got twenty minutes."

There was a silence before Mr. Mears yelled again. "Don't think you're getting away with this!" He shook his fist in my direction. Then his footsteps crunched back toward the plane.

I sighed with relief but decided not to look out yet. That was when I noticed the pain in my knee again. I bent over to examine it more closely. A dark gash ran from one side to the other. My leg and the hem of my dress were covered in blood. I had to stop the bleeding.

With my hanky I tied a bandage tightly over the cut. It did a pretty good job, so I gritted my teeth and straightened up. By leaning against the big rock for support, I peeked back at the runway.

Mr. Mears and Mr. Brown were talking with Uncle Harry. They shook hands with him, but I could see Uncle Harry shaking his head. He still didn't think the plane should be taking off. The two men climbed into their seats and Uncle Harry dropped the rope fence. Then he removed the chocks from in front of the wheels and ran back to the parked car to join Mr. Stevenson.

The plane blocked my view of the watchman's shack, but I pictured Jennie Mae and Pat crowded together at the window. Although this wasn't what I expected when I snuck out this morning, at least we would all see the takeoff. It was as if we were part of history.

The plane coughed and sputtered in the cold and puffs of smoke escaped the exhaust port. The smell of gasoline surrounded me. The engine caught and a thunderous roar made me cover my ears. It started to move. Within seconds it gathered speed and bounced down the runway. I clambered out of my little cave to see the takeoff better. My knee screamed with pain, but I didn't care.

The plane wobbled a bit, as if the wind got to it already. Then, just as it passed the end of the rocky ridge, the tail end lifted off the ground. For a split second I was about to cheer. Liftoff! But right away the plane swerved sharply to the left and then to the right.

Uncle Harry clenched his fists and put them up to his head.

The plane was out of control. But Mr. Brown managed to lift it off the ground. It wobbled something crazy in the strong wind. I covered my mouth with my hands to stifle a scream. Suddenly the engine cut out. After all the noise the silence was deafening. The wings dipped up and down. The plane quickly dropped. Before I could take another breath, the right wing caught the ground.

The City of New York somersaulted once, followed by the sound of splintering wood and flying gravel. I heard myself scream as it skidded into the rocks.

"Get out!" Uncle Harry shouted. "She'll burn!" He and Mr. Stevenson ran toward the plane.

I ran too—I couldn't stop myself. But my right leg wouldn't support me. In the middle of the runway, I fell and cried out in pain. I managed to roll onto one side and sit up just as Mr. Brown emerged through the hatch above the cockpit. Uncle Harry opened the door where Mr. Mears was sitting and pulled him out. Mr. Stevenson put his arm around Mr. Brown's waist and the four of them stumbled away from the plane.

Wait. Mr. Mears ran back. Tailwind! He was still in the plane. Mr. Mears reached the door, but Uncle Harry dragged him away.

"Hurry," I whispered. "Please, please hurry."

Mr. Mears struggled, but he was no match for Uncle Harry. He deposited him a good distance from the plane on the runway next to where Mr. Brown sat. Mr. Stevenson crouched beside them.

Uncle Harry ran toward me.

Over his shoulder he shouted back to the others. "I'll get the car."

I pulled my dress over my knees to hide the blood and waited for him. I couldn't get up, let alone run away to hide.

"My God, Ginny. What are you doing here?"

He reached down and pulled me to my feet.

"It crashed!" I replied. "Where's Tailwind?"

Uncle Harry held my shoulders and stared into my face.

"Are you all right?"

I nodded.

"Can you get yourself home?"

I nodded again.

He pointed me in the right direction, pushed gently on my back, and then ran toward the car.

CHAPTER FIVE

CONSEQUENCES

———◦———

I KEPT LOOKING back over my shoulder. The sky was blood-red. Not from an explosion—it was the morning sun, which peeked over the horizon.

I step-dragged toward the slope leading down from the airstrip. When I finally got there, the damp grass pulled my feet out from under me. I slid down the hill on my bottom. I lay there for a short rest and then pushed myself to my feet. I had to get home before everyone else got up.

At Stevenson's farm I leaned against the gatepost to catch my breath. As I looked around, something seemed to move in the rocks behind their house. But I didn't have the time or energy to investigate. To make matters worse the houses on Victoria Street seemed to move closer and then farther away. I shook my head to focus on the road and forced my feet to start moving again.

The rest of the walk was a blur until I was back on Water Street. I slid down the hill at the side of the store and slumped against the partly opened basement door. As it swung in, Llewellyn Crane jumped out of the way.

"You near scared me to death, Gin!" he said. Llewellyn was fifteen. He worked for Papa before and after school.

"Shhh." I put my finger to my lips. "I'm supposed to be up in my bed."

He smiled and nodded, but the smile disappeared when he saw the blood. He knelt on the dirt floor to take a closer look.

"I fell on the runway," I told him, leaving out the details about climbing into the plane.

"You're in some trouble, so you are." He stood up, pushed his long hair back, and looked me in the eyes.

"Please don't tell anyone, Llew."

"Your mother will have your hide."

"I'm going to sneak upstairs and clean up before anyone sees me."

"You're too late," he said. "Your papa asked me to come in at five this morning so we could clear the basement. The next shipment of supplies from Bowring Brothers arrives tomorrow. I've been carrying boxes up to him for at least half an hour."

That was when I noticed the sound of Papa's footsteps on the floor above us. I tried to think of a new plan, but the blood squishing around in my shoe told me I'd run out of time. I had no choice but to climb up to the store and face the consequences. I put one foot on the ladder and then collapsed in a heap on the dirt floor.

"Mr. Ross, help!" Llew dropped down on his knees in front of me. I heard Papa's footsteps running to the trap door.

"Say something, Gin." Llew leaned over me and put his hand on my shoulder. But I had no strength to answer him.

"Jesus, Mary, and Joseph!" Papa said from above. "Don't move her."

I heard him running to the front door. He wasn't taking a chance on that rickety ladder.

I was curled up on my side, my cheek resting on the damp earth. Llew brushed the hair off my face and held my hand.

"Help is on the way," he said. "You're going to be fine." Papa's panting announced his arrival at the basement door. He threaded his way through the crates and barrels.

Llew looked up. "She came in the back door, sir, but she hurt her knee. She can't climb the ladder." He got up to let Papa kneel down.

"Let's have a look at you." He put his arm behind my back and lifted me into a sitting position. My knee pounded with pain and my leg was a bloody, muddy mess.

"My God. What happened?" he asked.

"The City of New York crashed and—"

"What?"

"The plane, Mr. Ross," Llew said. "The one that landed at the airstrip yesterday."

"Good grief. And you were up there this morning?"

"We…I mean, I wanted to see her take off. But she crashed, and I ran with Uncle Harry to get them out."

"Ginny, Ginny." He gently held my face in his big hands. "Why do you insist on going up there?"

Tears ran down my cheeks.

He looked up at Llew. "Help me get her to the door, son, and I'll carry her to the store."

With their arms supporting me, I hopped out into the morning sun. Then Papa scooped me up in his arms and Llew ran ahead to open the front door. Once we were inside, Llew stood by the pot-bellied stove and Papa sat me on the long counter. He untied the hanky around my knee. The wound immediately filled up with blood. He shouted upstairs for Nana.

In her old bedroom slippers, Nana flapped down each stair until she was finally beside us. "Sweet Jesus. What has that girl done now?"

She wiped her floury hands on her apron and pinched the sides of the gash together. A thousand tiny knives cut into my knee. I tried not to cry out, but I couldn't hold back a moan. She let go and the edges popped apart. The knives cut deeper and I moaned again.

"That needs stitches." She looked up and shouted toward the stairs to tell Mom she'd better come down.

Billy, my six-year-old brother, arrived first.

"Yuck! How did that happen?"

"I fell."

"Where?"

"None of your business."

A big smile broke out on his face, and he ran to the bottom of the stairs to meet Mom. "I bet Ginny was at the airstrip again!"

I wondered, as I often did, why Billy was allowed to spoil his twelve-year-old sister's life.

Mom looked sternly at me. "Ginny?"

I looked at my lap.

"What have I told you about hanging around that airstrip?"

"Lots of people go up there to see the landings and takeoffs," Papa said.

"Lots of people are just curious," Mom replied. "Ginny is obsessed—drawings all over her room, following Uncle Harry around whenever he's up there—and this is the result!" She took her hand off her hip and pointed to the blood slowly dripping from my leg onto the floor. "If Billy wanted—"

Papa stepped between us and cut off the end of Mom's sentence. "I'll carry her to Doc Cron's before she bleeds to death," he said with a stern look.

Mom crossed her arms over her chest and shook her head. "Those damn planes," she mumbled.

CHAPTER SIX

TROUBLE

———◦———

P APA HUFFED AND puffed up Victoria Street with me in
his arms. There was no hospital in Harbour Grace, and
so everyone went to Doc Cron's house. He had two rooms
next to the side door for his patients. Pat and the rest of his
family lived in the other part of the house.

Uncle Harry and Mr. Mears were in the waiting room
when we arrived. I immediately looked down at the floor,
just in case Mr. Mears recognized me. Papa sat me on a chair
while Uncle Harry made introductions. I snuck a glance at
Mr. Mears. He looked pale and tired, with a gash on his
cheek and a huge lump on his forehead. Although his left
arm was in a sling, he stood up and shook Papa's hand.

"I'm glad to be alive to meet you, Joe," Mr. Mears said.

"I'm sorry about the crash, Henry," Papa replied. "Can you
salvage the plane?"

"Unfortunately, she's beyond repair."

As their conversation continued, Uncle Harry caught my

eye and frowned. He probably wondered what I was doing there, with blood covering my dress and running down my leg. I sure hoped he wouldn't ask me any questions in front of the others.

Before Mr. Mears slumped back in his chair, he told us that George Brown was still in with Doc Cron.

Uncle Harry and Papa sat down, and while the men talked my mind flashed back to my imaginary flight over Harbour Grace. I breathed in the cold air and saw the moon shining on the bay like a beacon leading due east to the Atlantic Ocean. I sat back and sighed with contentment.

But why had flying a plane suddenly become so important to me? A few weeks ago I was happy just to watch them from the ground and marvel at how they worked. The thought of being a mechanic, like Uncle Harry, was exciting enough for me.

Maybe it wasn't so much the thought of flying as the feeling of it. Sitting in Mr. Mears's plane was like nothing I'd ever felt before. It was so hard to put that feeling into words. Somehow I just felt comfortable there, as if I'd finally found the place where I belonged.

I snuck another glance at Mr. Mears. I knew his plane crashed, but he was fine. He was sitting right there. He raised his eyes and caught me looking at him.

"I want to be a pilot." The words came from somewhere deep inside me. Not from Ginny Ross but from the girl who soared over Joe Ross's store.

"What?" he asked.

I knew I should just keep my mouth shut, but I couldn't help myself. "I'm serious."

"Ginny, leave the poor man alone," Papa said.

Uncle Harry shook his head at me, but I couldn't stop.

"Really, Mr. Mears...sir."

This only got a chuckle out of him. "Get a safe job," he said. "An airplane is no place for a woman." He looked at the floor.

"Mr. Mears has just lost a lot of money," Uncle Harry said. "I'm sure he's not up to a conversation."

"To make matters worse," he said, still gazing at the floor, "I can't find my dog."

"Tailwind? I...." The words were out of my mouth before I had time to think about what I was saying.

Mr. Mears lifted his head. "How do you know the dog's name?"

"Uh, everyone is talking about you. You and Mr. Brown and the dog." I looked away. Uncle Harry raised his eyebrows and Papa looked puzzled. When I looked back at him, Mr. Mears stared right into my eyes.

"Just a minute now," he said. "Where did you hurt your knee?"

I didn't like the way the conversation was going. "I fell," I said. "In my yard. Uh, out back."

"Ginny Ross." Papa didn't look happy.

"I mean, I....." I looked at Uncle Harry for support, but he just shook his head.

"Now I get it," Mr. Mears said. "The girl at the airstrip walked with a limp."

He stood up and looked down at me. "Did you touch my plane?"

"I...I might have touched it. But just to put a good-luck charm on it."

Papa turned and looked at me, amazed.

"I knew it!" Mr. Mears said. "She touched something critical and caused the crash."

Before I could answer, Uncle Harry stood up. "Just a minute, Henry. It won't do to blame Ginny for your mistake. We warned you about those crosswinds and you ignored us."

Tears trickled down my face and my bottom lip trembled so much that I couldn't speak even if I wanted to. I looked up at Papa. He continued to watch Mr. Mears, but he slipped his hand around mine.

"It could've been the wind or it could've been somebody touching something she shouldn't have!" Mr. Mears said.

Just then the door to Doc's office opened and Mr. Brown limped out. "What's all the shouting about?" he asked.

"This is the one who was hanging around the plane!" Mr. Mears replied. "How do we know she's not responsible for the crash?"

"Come on, Henry," Mr. Brown said. "It was those damn crosswinds we tried to warn you about."

"How about a hot breakfast back at the hotel?" Uncle Harry asked. "You've already tasted my sister Rose's famous food." He looked from Mr. Mears to Mr. Brown, but neither was listening.

"We'll just see what the constable has to say about this," Mr. Mears said. "Come on, George."

When Mr. Brown didn't move, Mr. Mears gave him a furious look and slammed the door on his way out.

Mr. Brown sat down beside me. "What were you up to?"

I looked in his eyes, but I didn't see any anger there. Maybe it was time to tell the truth.

"I climbed into the plane and pretended I was flying over Harbour Grace."

Mr. Brown sighed and patted my hand. I was afraid to look at Papa and Uncle Harry.

CHAPTER SEVEN

GROUNDED

"NEVER MIND ALL that socializing!" Doc Cron shouted into the waiting room. "Get in here and let me do my work."

"We're leaving, Doc!" Uncle Harry called back.

"Take care, Miss Ginny." Mr. Brown looked at me with a kind of sadness in his eyes.

Papa picked me up again and deposited me on the examining table in the office. Doc Cron asked what happened, and once again I told my story of falling on the runway. He bent over to take a closer look at my knee. When he straightened up he looked at Papa and shook his head.

"This is going to be a big job, Joe," he said. "After I pick the gravel out and disinfect the wound, I have to trim the edges of the skin before I start stitching. Better let her squeeze your hands."

Those were the last words I heard. Doc's mouth moved as he worked, but the tiny knives cut so deeply I couldn't hear anything over my own moaning. I tried to squirm away, but Papa and Doc used their weight to pin me to the table.

Eventually the pain lessened and I opened my eyes. Papa still held both my hands in his.

"It's all over now, Ginny," Doc said. He continued wrapping my leg in a big white bandage. "Straight to bed with her, Joe. We don't want an infection."

Doc turned to me. "You wouldn't want to walk with a limp and a crutch for the rest of your life, would you? We'd have to call you Tiny Gin, like the boy in Charles Dickens's *A Christmas Carol.*" He laughed uproariously and ruffled my hair. The joke was pretty good, but I was too tired and sore to laugh.

After Papa carried me back home, he laid me on my bed. He sat down beside me and took my hand.

"Why didn't you tell me you climbed into the plane?"

"I didn't want you to be disappointed in me," I replied. "I know you don't want me to go near the planes, but I've made up my mind. I want to be a pilot."

"So I found out," he said. "And by the way, I'm not opposed to what you want to do with your life. I want you to have dreams, Ginny, but I don't want you to be disappointed. And I don't want you to get hurt."

I squeezed his hand. "I won't be."

"More importantly, I don't want you to lie to me."

"Never again." I crossed my heart and raised my right hand in the air.

He smiled and kissed my forehead, but Mom and Nana arrived and shooed him out before he could say anything else. In a few minutes I was in my nightgown with a pillow under my sore knee and Nana's red rose quilt wrapped around me. I pulled it up under my chin and closed my eyes.

That was the first time I'd stopped running since three o'clock in the morning. All I thought about was getting to the airstrip and then getting away. Even when I couldn't run with my legs, I ran in my mind. My body slowly relaxed and I sank into the warmth around me.

When I opened my eyes again, Mom was standing beside my bed. She held a couple of pillows and Nana stood beside her with my lunch tray. Billy sat on the end of the bed. Now that I wasn't bleeding all over the floor, the real lecture began.

"How many times have I told you to stay away from those planes?" Mom asked as she put one pillow behind my back and the other on my lap. "Planes are for men."

I kept my eyes on the corner of the quilt I was twisting around my finger.

"What's so special about those takeoffs?" She put her hands on her hips. A sure sign she meant business.

"It seems like a miracle that something so heavy can get off the ground."

"Well, I've got some miracles you can perform around this house," she said. "And that's what you'll be doing if you don't mark my words and stay away from that airstrip."

I felt Mom's eyes boring down on the top of my head.

"Am I understood?" she asked.

As I nodded, Nana put the tray on my lap. She reminded me to eat up so I wouldn't get an infected knee. Then she and Billy followed Mom to the door. Just as he got there, Billy turned around and stuck out his tongue. I picked up my spoon with a scowl on my face, and he scurried after them.

Maybe I couldn't say anything, but Mom couldn't stop me from thinking whatever I wanted. I knew women could do anything men could do. In fact, women had more sense than men. If I'd been flying Mr. Mears's plane, I wouldn't have crashed. I would have listened to Uncle Harry's advice.

I finished my boiled egg, dry toast, and tea. Mom said I had to eat lightly if I was just lying around in bed. Personally, I didn't see the logic in that. Hungry was hungry. What I really wanted was fish, brewis, and lassy toast. I moved the tray off my lap and closed my eyes again.

My stomach woke me with a series of rumbles and squeaks. I was looking around for some way of communicating with the kitchen when Papa stopped in for a visit. He sat on the edge of my bed and handed me a letter.

"More news from Toronto," he said.

"How is Dad?" I asked.

"Work is hard to find," he replied. "The money he makes at odd jobs pays for his room and meals at the boarding house. There is nothing left to send home."

"Why doesn't he go to Boston to work?" I asked. "Llewellyn's dad mails money to his family every week."

"He wouldn't want your other grandparents to know that things are tough down here."

"But Boston is a big place. He'd never run into Mom and Pop Davis."

Papa agreed with me and then laid the letter on my bedside table. He told me I could read it later because he was here to give me a pep talk. "I need you down in the store to go up the ladder and pass the tins down from the top shelves," he said. "And there are still bakeapples to pick and trout to catch in Rocky Pond."

I squeezed Papa's hand. "I'll be up and around before you know it."

He smiled and kissed my forehead. "You be sure you are," he said. "In the meantime, I'd better let you rest."

He got up, walked over to the window, and pushed it up. The screeching of the gulls down at Munn's wharf got louder. Sea air and the smell of salt cod filled the room. "If you can hear and smell what you're missing, you'll get better faster." He smiled at me from the end of my bed and blew me a kiss before walking downstairs to the store.

CHAPTER EIGHT

AMELIA EARHART

——◀◦▶——

"WAKE UP, Rip Van Winkle."

I opened my eyes and turned toward the voice. Pat sat in the wingback chair Papa had brought up from the parlour for visitors. I pushed myself up onto my elbows.

"Where have you been?" I asked. "I've been lying here for two days."

"You're lucky I'm here at all. Thanks to you, I missed the takeoff and the crash because Mr. Stevenson sent us home. Jennie Mae was in such a panic that I would try to sneak back to the airstrip, she stood at the end of our driveway until we heard the plane hit the ground. She ran home and I ran to the crash. By the time I got there, Mr. Stevenson was holding people away from the plane."

"Just a minute," I interrupted. "I've got my own complaint about you. You called Jennie Mae a farmer's brat."

"Oh, that," she answered. "I was mad at her, but I'm over it now."

I was puzzled by her lighthearted manner. Pat didn't usually recover so easily when someone made her angry.

"By the way, I forgive you, too," she said. "If you'd told me you were going to climb in the plane, I could have slipped away from Jennie Mae more easily."

Before I could explain that it was an impulse and not part of the plan, she took something cream-coloured out of her pocket. She handed it to me with a smile. I had to turn it over a few times before I realized it was a piece of the City of New York. Apparently she had found it in the gravel near where the plane had stopped.

"I can't wait to show it to Frank Murphy," she said.

"Why Frank Murphy?" I asked.

"He's tall like me and good-looking," she replied with another smile.

I was too stunned to answer. First she quickly forgave Jennie Mae and me. Then she couldn't wait to see Frank Murphy. He was as big a bully as Alice Brant. I knew Pat had been changing lately, but this was getting ridiculous.

She put the souvenir back in her pocket and leaned over to take her aviation scrapbook out of her school bag. By sharing her most prized possession, she showed me that she really had forgiven me. Still, she made me promise I wouldn't leave her out of any more adventures. I even had to cross my heart and hope to die if I broke my word.

She put the pillow for my meal trays on my lap and opened the book. I had seen it before, but this was the first time in a few months. She had information about all the Harbour Grace flights—from the Pride of Detroit in 1927 all the way up to the crash of the City of New York two days ago.

In a new section she had pasted everything she could find on Amelia Earhart. As I read, Amelia sprang to life in front of my eyes. She was no longer just a name I'd heard on the radio. I ran my finger over a picture of her in Burry Port, Wales, where she landed after her 1928 flight with William Stultz and Lou Gordon. She stood in the doorway of the plane, looking toward the crowd that was probably waving to her. She looked so relaxed and happy.

I had always been interested in how planes fly, but never in one particular pilot. Amelia Earhart was changing all that. I eagerly turned each page to read about her exploits and look at more pictures of her.

I turned to Pat. "She looks so tall when she's standing beside other people."

"Tall, slim, and beautiful," Pat agreed.

"Yes, I see that." Pat didn't say it, but I couldn't help thinking of how I looked in pictures: plump and plain.

"Look here!" Pat jumped up and leaned over the scrapbook. "Right now she's busy breaking records." The headlines from the *Boston Globe* read: **JUNE 25, 1930—EARHART SETS WOMEN'S SPEED RECORD** and **SEPT. 30, 1930—EARHART VICE PRES. OF NEW AIRLINE** and **APRIL 8, 1931—EARHART SETS WOMEN'S AUTOGIRO RECORD.**

"Can you imagine the thrill of flying a plane?" I asked.

"I'm not that crazy!" Pat replied.

"But you're so interested in planes, I thought—"

"Look. I like the drama and the excitement. But I don't like the danger. The only thing I want to be is famous." Pat put one hand behind her head and fluttered her eyelashes.

I giggled and shook my head. "And how are you going to accomplish that?"

"I'm not sure yet," she said. "But I'm working on it."

I didn't want to spoil her good mood by telling her I wanted to be a pilot. She might have thought I was trying to be more famous than her.

CHAPTER NINE

GUILT

THE NEXT MORNING Nana delivered my breakfast tray with a letter on it. I recognized Jennie Mae's handwriting. I'd been wondering where she was for the last three days. Even before I started my boiled egg and dry toast, I tore open the envelope.

Dear Ginny,

I don't want to come and see you. You lied to me. You and I were supposed to keep an eye on Pat but it was you I should have worried about. My dad is in big trouble. The constable came to our house. Mr. Mears said you touched his plane and that that caused the crash. My dad tried to say he didn't see you there but the constable interrupted.

He said he wasn't drawing any conclusions until he spoke to Mr. Brown and your Uncle Harry. I told you my dad would lose his job if any of us got caught.

Your former friend,
Jennie Mae Stevenson

P.S. Now I'm a liar too because I didn't tell my dad you were there.

My mouth suddenly felt dry and I had trouble swallowing. Tears filled my eyes. I pushed the tray off my lap and cried into the pillow so no one would hear me. Jennie Mae was right. I had made a mess of everything.

When I was all cried out, I ate my egg and toast. By the time my tea was gone, I knew what I had to do for Mr. Stevenson. I uncovered my legs and scooched to the edge of the bed. I felt a bit dizzy, but when I slid onto the floor, my legs held me. I limped to the window to give them a test run. Llew was in the backyard, walking from the storage shed to the basement door. I opened my window and he looked up.

"How are you feeling, Gin?"

I put my finger to my lips. "Fine," I whispered. "Can you take me out for a ride in Papa's delivery wagon?"

"If you ask him, I can."

"I'll meet you in front of the store as soon as I get dressed."

Ten minutes later I limped to the third-floor landing. Hanging on to the railing, I hopped down to the second floor. Fortunately Nana, Mom, and Billy were still in the kitchen. They were talking and I could hear the clink of dishes. I used the same method to get down the inside stairs to the store.

When Papa saw me, he rushed over.

"I said I wanted you back down here, but isn't this a bit too soon?" he asked.

"There's something I have to do, Papa. Can Llew use the delivery wagon to take me for a ride?"

Just then Llew walked in the front door. "If you agree, Mr. Ross, Ginny's carriage awaits."

Papa helped me to the front door and we both burst out laughing. Llew had Daisy—his big black Newfoundland dog—hooked up to the wagon. Papa took hold of my arm and helped me to step onto the wheel. I had a momentary flashback of stepping on the wheel cover to get into Mr. Mears's plane. But I pushed that picture out of my mind. There was work to be done.

After I sat down, Papa stepped back into the doorway. "Don't be too long."

He waved and I did the same.

Llew held onto Daisy's harness and the wheels squeaked as he walked down Water Street. Some of our neighbours smiled and waved when they saw me in the wagon. I did my best to smile and wave back, even though my mind was elsewhere.

"Where are we off to?" Llew asked.

"To the jail," I replied.

"Seriously?"

"I'm afraid this is very serious."

Llew continued to walk. He didn't press me for more details. He knew I would explain when I was ready. I tried to think of how I could tell him everything without admitting what I'd done to poor Mr. Stevenson. But I finally had to admit to myself that there was no way I could make this story sound any better. So I told him the whole truth.

"Whew. That really is serious," he said. Then he quickly added, "But I'll help you, Gin. You know I will."

I knew he would. Llewellyn had worked after school in the store since he was ten years old. Back then he swept the floor and stacked the shelves to earn money for his family. His dad worked out of town, so Llew was the man of the house. Now that he was fifteen and did most of the heavy work, Papa needed him more than ever. When Llewellyn Crane said he would do something, everyone knew he would.

We turned left onto Cochrane Street at the Archibald Hotel and headed up to Harvey Street. At the jail, Llew helped me out of the wagon and up the front stairs. When I opened the door, Constable Watts got up from his desk and walked over to us. "How is that leg of yours, Miss Ginny?"

Without answering, I grabbed his hand. "It's all my fault! Mr. Stevenson didn't know I was there—not because he wasn't doing his job. I tricked him. But I didn't cause the crash. You have to believe me."

"From what Ginny told me, the crosswind caused the crash," Llew said.

"Have you talked to Mr. Brown and Uncle Harry?" I asked. "They tried to warn Mr. Mears the winds were too unpredictable. But he refused to listen. I — "

"Calm down, Ginny." The constable patted my hand. "Mr. Brown leaves today, so he'll be in this morning with your Uncle Harry. I won't make any decisions until I talk with them." He shook my hand and thanked me for coming in.

Back at the wagon, Llew changed the subject. "Have you heard about Mr. Mears's dog?"

I swung around to face him. "Did they find him?"

"He's still missing. This morning on the radio, Mr. Mears offered a one-hundred-dollar reward to anyone who finds him."

"Llew, we have to go to the Stevensons' place! I think I know where Tailwind is."

As we approached the farm, the butterflies in my stomach swirled faster and faster. I remained in the wagon while Llew went to the door. Jennie Mae appeared and I waved to her. But she didn't wave back. She said a few words and closed the door.

For the second time today, my eyes filled up with tears. Llew returned to my side and handed me his handkerchief. I blew my nose and took a deep breath.

"Well, if she's not going to speak to me, you and I will have to find Tailwind ourselves. We'll split the reward and I'll give Mr. Stevenson my share. It's the least I can do since I'm the reason he'll probably lose his job."

Llew smiled and saluted.

"Right you are, Skipper!"

CHAPTER TEN

TAILWIND

————◁◦▷————

L LEW TURNED DAISY around and we walked away from the farm. I took one last look up the driveway and saw movement in one of the windows. Could it be someone waving? It was probably just wishful thinking, but I waved back, just in case.

There was a stand of trees between the house and the spot where I saw the movement in the rocks on the day of the crash. For our secret rescue operation, the trees offered good cover. As Llew helped me out of the wagon, we heard voices up at the airstrip. Just like us, others were looking for Mr. Mears's dog.

We walked quite a distance from the road before we got to the rocks. I was getting tired, so Llew found me a big stick to lean on. He walked slowly in front of the rocks and I limped along next to him.

"Call his name, Gin. He might recognize your voice from the plane."

"Tailwind, where are you?" I called and called, and after each calling, we stopped and listened for any sound.

After an hour or so, Llew gently touched my arm and suggested we return home. I didn't want to leave because this was my last chance to help Mr. Stevenson. But Llew was right. If Tailwind were here, then we would have heard something by now. I reluctantly walked back to the wagon and Llew helped me in.

He gave Daisy's harness a little tug, but she didn't move. "Come on," he said.

Again she didn't move. He pulled harder, but she just dug her feet into the gravel and leaned away from him. He looked at me and shrugged.

Then he bent over and picked up her front paw. "Maybe she has a stone stuck in her foot."

But there was nothing there. He picked up her other front paw, but still nothing. When he picked up her back paw, he burst out laughing. Before I could ask him what was so funny, he got down on his stomach and crawled under the wagon. I leaned over the side to see him wriggle out with a grey bundle in his arms.

"It's Tailwind!" I held out both hands and Llew passed him to me. He was damp and shivering. In fact, he didn't even look like the dog we'd seen before the crash. I snuggled him in my arms and he licked my neck. I laughed and petted him.

"He's thanking you for finding him," Llew said. "And we

have to thank you, too, old girl." He scratched Daisy's big head. "You're the smartest dog in the whole world!"

In minutes we were back at the farm. Jennie Mae ran down the driveway with a huge smile on her face.

"Dad didn't lose his job!" she shouted.

I heaved a sigh of relief and in my mind thanked Constable Watts for his quick investigation.

Then Jennie Mae saw Tailwind and clapped her hands.

"You'll get the reward."

"Since I caused your dad so much worry, I want him to have my share," I said.

"He'd never take your money," Jennie Mae replied.

I waved Llew over and whispered in his ear. He smiled and nodded.

"Since we found Tailwind on your property, you should take one third of the reward," I said. "And we won't take no for an answer."

Llew put his arm around Jennie Mae's shoulders and took hold of Daisy's harness.

"Off we go, ladies," he said. "We've got a reward waiting for us!"

All the way along Harvey Street and then down Cochrane Street, we talked about what we would do with our share of the one hundred dollars. If her parents didn't need all of her money, Jennie Mae wanted to put some aside for Teachers' College in St. John's. Llew planned to give most of his money to his mom, but he would keep some to buy what he needed to go to sea—not as a fisherman, but as a sailor in the merchant fleet. He wanted to take salt cod from Newfoundland to the Caribbean Islands and bring back rum, fresh fruit, and molasses.

"I'm going to use some of my money to become a pilot," I told them.

"Wow!" Jennie Mae said. "You know enough about planes, that's for sure."

Llew stopped and shook my hand. "I'm with Jennie Mae. If anyone can do it, it's you, Gin."

CHAPTER ELEVEN

REWARD

———◦———

THE ARCHIBALD HOTEL was a two-storey brick building on Water Street, about a five-minute walk from Papa's store. All the pilots, plane owners, and mechanics stayed there when they were in Harbour Grace for a transatlantic crossing.

Llew, Jennie Mae, Tailwind, and I walked into the hotel. We heard laughter coming from the dining room. Jennie Mae told me to go in first, but I wasn't so sure that was a good idea. I knew Mr. Mears would be glad to see Tailwind, but I didn't know if he would be glad to see me. I peeked around the corner to see which way the wind was blowing.

Uncle Harry and Mr. Mears sat at one of the tables with their backs to the door. Aunt Rose stood in front of them doing an impersonation of Doc Cron. She stuck out her stomach and spoke in a gruff voice. "I don't care if you have to make bread for lunch, madam. Kindly clear off that table so I can remove your husband's appendix."

The men burst out laughing again.

Uncle Harry lifted his teacup into the air. "To my sister Rose Archibald, the best impersonator in Harbour Grace."

Mr. Mears raised his cup too. "To the best impersonator in all of Newfoundland."

This seemed like a good time to slip into the room. I took a deep breath and nodded to the other two. Jennie Mae took Llew's hand and we moved forward together.

"Well, look who's here," Aunt Rose said.

Mr. Mears turned around and jumped up so quickly his chair crashed to the floor. Tailwind squirmed in my arms with excitement. When I handed him over, Mr. Mears cuddled the dog to his chest.

"Where did you find him?"

Jennie Mae stepped forward. "Ginny and Llewellyn found him."

"Actually, Ginny figured out where he was," Llew said. "I just helped her get there."

"But we're going to split the reward three ways," I added. There was silence for a few seconds while Mr. Mears continued to pat Tailwind. Aunt Rose looked him in the eye. "A thank-you might be appropriate," she said.

"Yes.... Yes, of course. Thank you," Mr. Mears replied. "Please, sit down—all of you."

I told him he was welcome and then described where we found Tailwind.

"But how did you know to look there?"

I was afraid he would ask this question. "Well, now." I

cleared my throat. "I hate to bring this up, but—when I was leaving the airstrip the morning of the crash, I thought I saw something move in the rocks at Stevensons' farm." I leaned forward on my chair. "I just heard he was missing a few hours ago, or I would have told someone sooner."

"He's home now and that's all that matters," he said.

Mr. Mears excused himself to get the reward money and took Tailwind with him. We heard him murmuring baby talk to the dog as he carried him toward the stairs.

"Pull your chairs up to the table, my pets, and I'll get some tea and blueberry pie," Aunt Rose said.

Uncle Harry stayed where he was. He loved anything with blueberries in it.

Lilly Shanahan came out of the kitchen with a big pot of tea.

"The three of you are some lucky to be getting the reward," she said. "Especially in these hard times."

Lilly worked part-time for Aunt Rose, mainly in the kitchen. She was fifteen and finished school, but she and I always visited when I came to the hotel. She walked around the table and filled our cups.

"Have you hooked any more of those beautiful rugs?" I asked. She showed them to me whenever I saw her.

"I have an order from Miss Rorke, the new teacher, for three of them," Lilly said. "Do you think your papa would give me some burlap sacks to use as the backings?"

"I'm sure he will."

She smiled, thanked me, and returned to the kitchen for the pie.

I waited until Uncle Harry had eaten the last blueberry on his plate before I asked the question that had been puzzling me. "I was so afraid the plane would catch fire when it crashed. What saved it?"

"The extra gas tank was welded into the frame so well that it didn't budge. The fact that the plane landed on its belly prevented the gas tanks in the wings from rupturing."

"That was a blessing," Aunt Rose said as she walked in with another pot of tea.

Mr. Mears returned. He gave Tailwind to me. Then he walked around the table to hand each of us thirty-five dollars in American money. He explained he didn't have thirty-three dollars and thirty-three and one third cents for each of us. We all laughed and thanked him.

"Thanks to you three, my little friend and I can return to New York tomorrow."

I smiled at Mr. Mears and he smiled back.

"I...." He sat down at the table and I passed Tailwind to him. "I'm sorry I blamed you for the crash, Ginny," he said. "I could say I was tired and upset, but there's no excuse for what I did." He looked over at Jennie Mae and asked her to apologize to her dad for him. She smiled shyly and nodded.

"Well, I'm glad that's all cleared up," Aunt Rose said.

We put our money in our pockets and stood up to leave.

"Could I speak to you for a minute, Mr. Mears?" I asked.

Uncle Harry reminded Aunt Rose that they should go over the accounts. She agreed and they both left. Llew and Jennie Mae decided to check on Daisy. When the room was empty, I sat down and faced Mr. Mears.

"I really do want to be a pilot."

He smiled and shook his head. "What can I say to you?" he asked. "You just saved my dog's life." He hesitated for a few seconds and then looked into my eyes. "I have to be honest, Ginny. Becoming a pilot is almost impossible. I know you're brave—and stubborn—but the odds are against you."

CHAPTER TWELVE

THE GIFT

—◄◦►—

O N THE STEPS of the Archibald Hotel, I kissed Tailwind's head one last time before I climbed back into the wagon. In spite of our first meeting, I had come to like the little fellow.

Mr. Mears waved and Tailwind wagged his tail. Llew grasped Daisy's harness and we walked toward the store. I blinked back the tears and told them what Mr. Mears had said.

Llew turned around. "You'll make him eat his words, Gin. Just you wait and see."

"I'll say," Jennie Mae added. "You won't crash like he did!"

I brushed away the tears and smiled up at the two of them. My head told me Mr. Mears was probably right. But my heart told me not to give up. I had never been happier than when I sat in that plane. I just knew I wanted to feel that way again.

I put my hand in my pocket and fingered my thirty-five-dollar reward. It was comforting to know I had made a good start toward saving for my flying lessons.

Thinking about the reward reminded me of what Lilly had said.

"Why is the reward a blessing in these hard times?" I asked.

"It's the Depression," Llew said.

"I remember hearing that word on the radio," Jennie Mae said. "Something about banks closing and people losing all their money."

"In the newsreels at the Masonic Hall, I saw men without jobs lining up by the dozens for a bowl of soup and a piece of bread," I said. "But that's in Canada—not here."

"Wait until the fishermen, sealers, and whalers can't pay their bills at the store," Llew said. "If they aren't being paid, they can't pay your papa."

"Does Papa know about this?"

"Of course," Llew replied. "And he's very worried."

We talked some more, and I found out the Stevensons were doing fine because of their farm. They only needed to buy a few staples like flour, sugar, and salt. The Cranes got money from Llew's dad, who worked in the shipyards in Boston. Together with what Llew made in the store, they got by.

Now that I thought about it, maybe the Depression affected Uncle Harry. He had been the accountant at the

Archibald Boot and Shoe Factory, but it went bankrupt a few years ago. Now he had to live with Aunt Rose and take care of her accounts, as well as the airstrip.

When we rounded the curve on Water Street, Papa was standing outside the store. He waved at us to hurry. I waved back and Llew, Daisy, and Jennie Mae broke into a run.

Papa rushed up to the wagon. "Where have you been? I've been worried sick!"

"We found Tailwind and got the reward," I told him.

"Lord love us," Papa said. He helped me out and gave me a big hug. When he released me, I walked over to Daisy and snuggled her big black head to thank her for pulling me around town. She responded with a lick that covered half my face. I thanked Llew, too.

He took my hand and shook it. "If it wasn't for you, I wouldn't have my share of the reward."

Jennie Mae thanked me with a kiss on the cheek and then announced she wanted to get home to give her parents her money. Llew wanted to do the same. He released Daisy from the wagon, and the three of them walked down Water Street.

Once we were in the store I got the same *where have you been* from Mom and Nana. Fortunately, the news about the reward put any thoughts of punishment for my lateness out of their heads.

The two customers in the store shook my hand, patted me on the back, and congratulated me. I thanked them, and they hurried out the door. If I knew Mrs. Parsons and Mrs. Duff, the story of our reward would be all over town in an hour. Another thought hit me. Pat! I had forgotten all about my cousin. I would have to explain that getting the reward wasn't another adventure without her. But right now I had to speak to Papa. I walked to the long counter where he was opening a box of hard bread.

"I want you to have some of my money," I said.

"Oh, I couldn't, Ginny. You earned it and you should keep it."

Nana walked from the back of the store to stand beside him. She put her hand on his arm. "It will pay for the next shipment from Bowring Brothers," she reminded him.

Papa stood still for a few seconds. I knew he was thinking. "I'll take fifteen dollars and you take twenty dollars for yourself," he said.

I wondered if his share would pay for a whole shipment. "I'll take ten dollars and you take twenty-five," I replied.

He hesitated and then leaned over the counter to shake my hand.

"Deal."

That made me feel good. I got to help Papa and I had the first ten dollars toward my flying lessons. I handed him the money and he handed me my share. Before I could put it back in my pocket, Mom leaned over my shoulder and plucked it from my hand. How she got from behind the short counter so quickly, I'll never know.

"This will do very nicely for the material I need to sew our new winter coats."

I whirled around to face her. "But I don't want—"

She gave me a look that said *one more word and you'll regret it.* But I didn't care.

"I'm the one who earned the money, not you!"

Mom's eyes blazed and she stepped toward me. But I didn't back away. I stood there waiting for the slap I expected was coming. For some reason, she hesitated. She stuck her finger in my face and whispered through her clenched teeth. "Don't ever speak to me that way again." She turned to walk away.

"Wait," Papa said to her. "You won't need all her money for material. At least give her a few dollars back."

"Since when did you become the expert on sewing?" she asked. "I think I know the cost of material, thank you." She folded the bills and put them in her pocket.

Papa sighed and shook his head.

I figured it was a good time to leave, so I walked up the inside stairs. "You may have my money," I whispered. "But you can't stop me from making a new plan for my flying lessons."

CHAPTER THIRTEEN

LETTER

———◦———

L ATER THAT NIGHT, when everyone was in bed, I put my new plan into action. With my quilt wrapped around me, I snuck back downstairs. I turned on the kitchen light and waited to see if Nana or Papa stirred in their bedroom next door. When I was sure the coast was clear, I took Nana's paper, straight pen, and bottle of ink out of the drawer in the kitchen table. With my back to the stove, I began to write.

Dear Miss Earhart,

My name is Ginny Ross and I'm almost thirteen years old. I live in Harbour Grace, Newfoundland, where most of the transatlantic flights take off. I don't know if you answer letters, but I would be very grateful if you answered this one.

You see, I have a problem. I want to be a pilot like you, but I don't have anyone to teach me how to fly.

My Uncle Harry is the airport supervisor and he knows a lot about mechanics. He has books on the subject that he loans me. With his supervision I can clean the spark plugs, change the oil, and replace the old air filter on my Aunt Rose's car. So you can see I'm in training already.

My papa (grandfather) thinks I should follow my dream to be a pilot. My friends, Jennie Mae and Llewellyn, say if anyone can do it, it's me. I think this proves there are people who know I'm serious about my dream and believe in me.

I know I have to finish school, so my goal for now is to make all the arrangements for my flying lessons. Then, when I graduate, everything will be in place for me to learn how to fly.

I really hope you can help me, Miss Earhart. I'll work very hard and do everything you suggest.

Your admirer,
Ginny Ross

I read the letter over a few times before putting it in an envelope. With the writing supplies back in the drawer, I turned off the light and returned to my room. For some time I lay awake thinking about where to send my letter and whose name I could use on the return address. If I got a reply from Amelia Earhart, Mom would destroy it before I had a chance to see it.

The next morning I gobbled down my breakfast and hurried down to the store. I could hear Papa and Llew in the basement, but I didn't have time to say hello. There were only a few more days of summer holidays, and I wanted to get my letter in the mail before school started.

Just as I opened the front door, Doc Cron arrived. "Time to take a look at those stitches, Ginny."

I sighed and sat down on the stool next to the stove.

"Don't give me that pouting," he said. "Whatever you have to do can wait."

In my head, I yelled, *No, it can't! My whole future depends on mailing this letter.*

As if this delay wasn't bad enough, he had to go upstairs to wash his hands and get Nana to help him. The next sound I heard was her slippers flapping slowly down the stairs. She and Doc were deep in conversation about how lucky I was that I didn't develop an infection.

"I guess we won't have to call her Tiny Gin after all," Doc said. It felt as if this process was going to take all morning.

"All right, my ducky," Nana said. "Let's see what we have here." She cut the tape on the gauze and started to unravel the bandage. "I'm sure the Egyptian mummy makers didn't do as thorough a job as Doc Cron."

Finally, the bloodstained piece of gauze over the wound was exposed. Doc peeled it away. "That looks beautiful!" he said.

All I could see were black stitches surrounded by puffy red skin. I started to get up, but Doc pulled me back down onto the stool. He wasn't finished poking, prodding, and discussing his handiwork. Nana was our in-house medical person, and she kept asking question after endless question.

"Let's see you walk," Doc said.

At last! I got up and stiff-kneed my way to the front door.

"Bend that knee, girl, or it will stiffen up permanently," Doc shouted.

I turned back to blow them a kiss and hurried out the door. Lilly Shanahan jumped out of my way. She was probably here for her burlap sacks. I smiled and told her they were behind the short counter. Nana would get them for her.

Then, at last, I was free. I limped down to the *Harbour Grace Standard* office to get the address for the *Boston Globe.* It was the newspaper Pat used for the stories about Amelia Earhart in her scrapbook. If this paper wrote stories about Amelia, maybe they knew where she lived and would forward my letter.

Mr. Butt, the editor, smiled when I walked in the door.

"What can I do for Miss Ross this morning?" he asked.

"I need an address for the *Boston Globe,*" I replied.

"Why do you need that?"

"Ah...Uncle Harry needs it."

Telling the lie gave me a sense of heat crawling up my neck. Fortunately, Mr. Butt turned to the filing cabinet before my face was completely red. He fingered through a number of files before he wrote something on a slip of paper. He handed it to me and told me to say hello to Uncle

Harry for him. I got out of there before I started blushing again.

The experience gave me more than an address for the *Globe.* It gave me the name and return address for my letter. Uncle Harry encouraged me to learn all I could about mechanics and, more importantly, he could keep a secret.

The post office was quiet when I got there. I walked to one of the desks and sat down. My letter needed a P.S., so I slipped it out of the envelope. I dipped the pen in the inkwell and wrote:

P.S. The name on the return address is my Uncle Harry's. I can't use my own address because my mother thinks planes are for men only.

I addressed the envelope and waited until Mr. Godden, the postmaster, was free.

"Why is your Uncle Harry writing to Amelia Earhart?" he asked.

"Oh, you know Uncle Harry," I said vaguely.

"I certainly do," he said. "He's a man of many interests."

For the rest of the day, I pictured my letter floating through the air from Harbour Grace to Port aux Basques and then on to Boston. I saw Amelia sitting in the sunlight at her desk and writing a reply. Her letter took the same route back to Harbour Grace, just like the lines drawn on a map at the beginning of the adventure movies at the Masonic Hall.

CHAPTER FOURTEEN

SCHOOL

IT WAS THE first day of school and I sat by the pot-bellied stove admiring my knee. Doc Cron took out the stitches last night, and all that remained was a raised red scar. I was all ready to start grade eight. I pulled my dress over my legs and looked around. Papa was in his usual place behind the long counter, and Billy, Mom, and Nana were still upstairs.

Before I could start a conversation with Papa, Uncle Harry rushed in the front door. "Since you're up and about, I think it's time you came back to helping me repair Aunt Rose's car."

Until the crash, I'd been going to her garage behind the hotel most afternoons. Uncle Harry said girls should know the mechanics if they wanted to learn how to drive a car. Now that I was going to be a pilot, I realized my mechanics lessons were even more important. I hoped he would teach me how the engines of cars and planes were similar.

"I'll expect to see you at ten after four," he said from the open door.

I gave him the okay sign just as Billy stomped down the inside stairs. "I don't see why I have to go to school," he said.

"Because you're six years old, and all six-year-olds have to go to school," I replied.

"You should be happy to start your education," Papa said.

"But I want to play with my friends."

"Where do you think they'll be this morning?" I asked.

Billy stomped over to the stove and flopped down on the chair next to me. Mom told him he had to hold my hand to walk to school on the first day, and he was not happy about that, either.

The clock in the parlour struck eight and it was time to leave. I walked behind the counter to kiss Papa goodbye. Now that I saw him up close, he looked pale and his skin was damp. I reached up and touched his face.

"Don't you be fussing over me," he said. "It's just my indigestion playing up again. Off you two go."

For the first time since we were in grade one, Pat wasn't waiting for me in front of her house. I wanted to explain to her that I didn't plan to find Tailwind without her. But I hadn't had time to look for her. As soon as I got to school, I would straighten things out.

Jennie Mae rushed up to us at the gate. Billy immediately dropped my hand and ran into the schoolyard without me. It was probably a good thing, because as soon as I walked in, I was swamped by people.

"Show us your scar, Ginny."

"Where did you find Tailwind?"

"How did you know where to look?"

When I couldn't answer the questions quickly enough, some people started to ask Jennie Mae for the details. Those in front of me pushed closer, and there was no way I could look for Pat.

But as quickly as the crowd arrived, now it was leaving. I looked beyond the faces next to me and saw Alice Brant and some of the other grade nines walking toward us. The grade ones parted like the Red Sea in front of them. Then Alice and I were face to face. The only one left beside me was Jennie Mae.

"I hear you two got the reward for finding that dog," Alice said.

"Yes, we did," I replied.

"Why does a fat, ugly girl like you need money?" she asked. "It can't improve how you look."

I bit my tongue and tried to stare her down.

"What about the farmer's brat?" Alice continued.

Jennie Mae stood her ground but didn't answer.

"Dog got your tongue?" Alice taunted Jennie Mae. Her friends laughed at the joke, and then Alice pushed Jennie Mae.

"Maybe you should mind your tongue." I stepped toward Alice, and the next thing I saw were stars. When they cleared, I saw Alice and Jennie Mae in a clinch. Each was punching at the other with her free hand. The grade nines stood in a circle around them and egged Alice on. I wiped the blood from under my nose and moved forward to help Jennie Mae.

Suddenly, everyone was swinging, pushing, and shouting. All I could see were eyes and mouths and hands. Then I heard a familiar voice.

"All right, you lot! That's enough." It was Llewellyn.

I could see him because he was taller than the rest of the crowd. But before he could get close enough to help us, Frank Murphy swung him around. I lost sight of them when someone punched me in the side of the head.

A big brass bell rang, and we all stopped. A group of teachers walked toward us. Miss Davis grabbed Jennie Mae by the elbow, and Mr. Shepherd, the principal, took hold of Frank Murphy's shirt. Mrs. Alley had me by the arm. They marched us toward the school, and that's when I noticed Pat leaning on the wall next to the door. As we passed through it, she whispered, "How does it feel to be famous now?"

How could I have been so dumb? The problem wasn't finding Tailwind or getting the reward without her. She wanted all the attention that we got. Maybe it was supposed to be the first step on her road to becoming famous. I wondered if Pat and I could ever be friends again.

In the doorway to our classroom, Miss Rorke met Jennie Mae and me. She sent us to the girls' bathroom to wash our face and hands. We looked at each other in the mirror over the sink.

"We all know Alice is a bully, but what made her pick on us in particular?" Jennie Mae asked.

"Pat," I replied. Then I told her what Pat had said when I walked into the school.

Jennie Mae just shook her head. "That's one bad partnership!" she said.

I buttoned up my sweater to cover the drops of blood on my white blouse, and we walked back to class. The rest of the morning passed with us looking at two names on the blackboard—*Detentions: Ginny Ross and Jennie Mae Stevenson.* Every time I sneaked a glance at Pat, she avoided looking at me. I wondered if she felt sorry for what she had done.

At noon I asked Billy to tell Mom I was going to Jennie Mae's for lunch. Her sisters wouldn't tell on her.

"And if you tell on me, you'll regret it." I shook my finger under Billy's nose like Mom did. He pulled away from me and ran through the school gate laughing.

CHAPTER FIFTEEN

MORE TROUBLE

———◦———

I WAS SUPPOSED to be at Aunt Rose's at ten after four to work on her car. By the time my detention was over, it was 4:40 P.M. I ran into the garage to find Uncle Harry, dressed in his coveralls, with his head under the hood of Aunt Rose's Model T Ford. I explained why I was late, and his eyebrows hitched up the way they did when he was surprised. I waited for him to say something, but he just shook his head. I'm sure he knew what would happen to me when I got home.

"Is it too late for my lesson?" I asked. A change of subject seemed like a good idea.

"I'm finished for today, but I'll show you how to change the brake fluid next time we meet." His smile showed he wasn't angry about my lateness.

I took my time getting home. I was pretty sure Billy had told on me, and there was no need to hurry into Mom's anger. Nervously, I opened the front door.

Papa was the only one in the store. Llew was probably out back or in the basement. Mom and Nana were probably upstairs.

I sighed with relief and walked over to the long counter where Papa was standing. "How's your indigestion?"

"All gone, thanks." He gave my hand a quick squeeze.

"I guess you heard about what happened at school."

"I'm afraid so," he said. "You better stay away from your mother for now."

I snuck up the inside stairs and paused outside the kitchen door to see if I was the topic of conversation. Through the crack between the open door and door frame, I saw Mom sitting at the kitchen table chopping vegetables and Nana stirring a big pot on the wood stove.

"It seems we're cooking more wild game and fish these days," Nana said. The delicious smell of rabbit stew filled the hallway.

"No one has any money," Mom replied. "They're paying for their groceries with whatever they can grow or catch."

"It's a good thing Ginny gave Papa some of her reward money to pay for our last shipment from Bowring Brothers," Nana said. "I doubt that they'll accept chickens, rabbits, vegetables, and fish the next time we have to pay them."

I crept up to the third floor and sat at the top of the stairs. With my head against the wall, I thought about the Depression again. Then there was the fight at school and my detention to worry about. I decided to think of something pleasant, instead.

With my eyes closed I imagined I was flying out over the bay. The sun shone brightly in the cloudless sky and diamonds shimmered on the surface of the water. Four fishing schooners swayed gently at anchor. And there was Llew on our wharf passing supplies down to a fisherman in a dory. I tipped my wings and they both waved up at me.

Laughter on the inside stairs brought my daydream to an end. Papa and Uncle Harry were on their way up. I tiptoed back down to the second-floor landing. Nana directed Uncle Harry to Dad's chair. When everyone was seated, I walked in and sat down.

"What was this fighting all about?" Mom asked me.

Before I could answer, Billy explained. "Alice Brant said the reward money wouldn't make Ginny look any better."

"That Brant girl has some mouth on her," Uncle Harry said.

"Never mind Alice Brant!" Mom cut in. She turned her glare from Uncle Harry to me. "It's those damn planes again."

"Finding Tailwind was an act of kindness," Papa said. "It had nothing to do with planes."

"If she hadn't been at the airstrip the morning of the crash, she wouldn't have known where to find that dog," Mom pointed out.

"Ginny got a d—" Billy added.

"Don't interrupt me," Mom snapped at him. She turned back to me. "What am I going to do with you? You can't even go to school without making a spectacle of yourself."

"It seems to me there were a lot of people making spectacles of themselves," Papa said.

"Ginny is my concern, thank you," Mom replied. "And she won't be going out with her friends for the next month," she added. "Straight to school and straight back home." She picked up her fork and pointed it in my direction. "Planes are for men! If you ever forget that again, you'll regret it."

Papa sighed and picked up his fork. No one moved until Uncle Harry put a big forkful of stew in his mouth. "No one does up a rabbit like you, Nana," he said with a smile.

Others dug into their stew and the conversation around the table slowly resumed. Uncle Harry accepted a second helping, but Papa rubbed his chest and shook his head. "Darn indigestion again," he said. "I think I'll just finish up with some tea."

In a few minutes the men had left the table, and I asked to be excused to do my homework. Billy started to speak again, but a look from Nana shut him up. I hurried out in case he decided to add more to what he had already said.

From the second-floor landing I heard Uncle Harry and Papa talking in the store. I slipped down the inside stairs until I could see them. They sat beside the stove. Papa slouched down in his chair, with his feet stretched out in front of him and his arms crossed on his chest. Uncle Harry stared into the fire through the open door, with his elbows resting on his knees.

"I'm worried about Ginny," he said. "Can you imagine what will happen when more people find out she wants to be a pilot?"

"I worry about her, too, Harry. But what else has she got to look forward to around here? She's not exactly the kind of daughter her mother wants."

Uncle Harry chuckled. "You're right about that. She doesn't sing, dance, or play the piano like the other girls, and she couldn't care less about clothes."

"If she wants to be a pilot, then I'll support her any way I can," Papa said.

Uncle Harry sat up and clasped his hands behind his head. "I don't mind teaching her the mechanics of a car, Joe. But her chances of becoming a pilot are so slim, I'm afraid to encourage her."

Papa puffed on his pipe. "That's up to you, Harry."

I tiptoed back up the stairs to my room and started my homework. But I kept thinking about what Uncle Harry said. He was right about the things I couldn't do, and there were others. I didn't care about sewing, painting, or table manners. Maybe that's why I wanted to be a pilot. I was looking for something—anything—I could be good at. I closed my arithmetic book and started to draw a Lockheed Vega.

An hour later I heard Papa entering his bedroom. I hurried to the grate in the floor next to my bedside table. "Is that you, Papa?" I whispered.

He walked to the grate and looked up at me with a big smile. "Is someone on my private telephone?"

I smiled back at him. "Thank you, Papa."

"What for?" he asked.

"For supporting my dream."

"Eavesdropping again, were you?"

"You know me."

Papa chuckled. "Yes I do—and I also know how stubborn you are," he said. "If you've made up your mind to be a pilot, that's good enough for me."

"I love you, Papa."

He blew me a kiss and moved away from the grate. I did the same and returned to my desk. I had to find some way to convince Uncle Harry I had what it took to be a pilot. If he thought my chances were too slim to encourage me, what would he do with Amelia's letter when it arrived?

CHAPTER SIXTEEN

INVENTION

WITH THE OUTSIDE door to the basement open, the bright sunshine flooded in. I knew exactly what I needed, but where to find it was the question. The light was best near the door, so I looked there first. No luck. I slowly made my way through the barrels to the back wall. And there was exactly what I needed—a wooden crate about two feet wide and three feet long.

"Hi, Gin. What are you doing down here?" Llew appeared over my left shoulder.

"I need this, but it needs to be altered." I lifted the crate and put it down in front of him. "If I push out the bottom and then cut out one side, I can put it on the table and sit inside it."

"I think I know what you're up to," Llew said.

He smiled and carried the crate to the doorway. As he started to push out the bottom, I told him I had to do it myself. He offered to get me a hammer and saw to make the job easier. Every now and then he stopped his own work to watch me or to hold the crate while I sawed.

In half an hour I was finished, but I couldn't leave it there. Uncle Harry's aviation books were at the Archibald Hotel. I sneaked through the back gardens along the sea side of Water Street with the crate over my shoulder. When I got opposite the hotel, I looked both ways, crossed the street, and banged my way in the front door. I went directly to the kitchen and bumped through the swinging door.

"What's this?" Aunt Rose asked. She wiped her hands on her apron and walked over to the crate.

"I'm making a surprise for Uncle Harry," I replied. "Can I work in your basement?"

"He rarely goes down there, so it should be a safe place for you," she said. "May I ask what this humble crate will become?"

"It's a surprise."

Lilly dried her hands and joined us. She examined the crate from every side. "Well, I'm sure I can't guess what it is."

"Then you'll all be surprised."

Aunt Rose opened the basement door and pulled the cord that turned on the light. I bumped the crate down the stairs, but I wasn't sure where I should put it. The basement was filled with furniture sitting on wide wooden planks on the dirt floor. It was the storage area for what Aunt Rose wasn't using in the hotel.

I looked up at her and she walked down the stairs. She pointed to her right. "Follow this little aisle," she said. "At the end, turn left and you'll find a dining room table."

I followed her directions, and there it was.

"Can I put my crate on it?" I asked.

"I'll get you an old blanket to protect the table—and then you can," she replied.

With my project safely hidden, I headed up to the Stevensons' farm. It was Saturday and Jennie Mae had chores. We arranged to meet in front of the hotel when she was finished.

At three o'clock, Jennie Mae stood looking at the crate. I pulled up a chair, leaned into it, and touched the end.

"I don't get it," she said.

I moved my fingers to specific points and made the sound of an engine starting up.

"You're going to learn to drive your Aunt Rose's car?"

I made louder noises and bounced up and down on the chair. Jennie Mae frowned but said nothing. I pushed forward on an imaginary throttle and threw myself against the back of the chair.

"You're going to learn to fly a plane!" She clapped her hands with glee. "Can I help?"

"Why do you think you're here?"

She pulled up another chair and sat right beside me. I opened one of Uncle Harry's aviation books to a diagram of the cockpit in a Lockheed Vega. Together, Jennie Mae and I plotted where each instrument would appear in my plane.

"I think you should draw the dials and switches in pencil first," Jennie Mae said.

"And then I can paint them black," I added. "Aunt Rose paints scenes around Harbour Grace. Maybe she'll loan me some black paint and a brush."

"That will look amazing," Jennie Mae said.

I wasn't very good at drawing circles, so Jennie Mae found me the lids from various empty jars stored in the basement. She also held the aviation book open so I had both hands free to draw.

My month of going straight home after school was over, and so we went to the hotel every day. In a week, my cockpit looked very similar to the one in the book. Now it was time for the paint.

I went to Aunt Rose and she agreed to loan me what I needed. She also suggested I paint over the advertising on the outside of the crate. I couldn't have her watercolours for that job, but she gave me some white house paint and a big brush.

"Can I paint the outside?" Jennie Mae asked.

She had been such a loyal assistant. It was the least I could do.

"Sure," I replied.

We had to let the house paint dry for three days before we could continue. Painting the dials and switches was the hardest job. Again, Jennie Mae suggested I use the jar lids to trace over the pencil outlines. This helped to steady my hand and make neat painted circles. Another two days and our masterpiece was finished.

We waited until Uncle Harry was sitting in the kitchen with Aunt Rose and Lilly. I carried my cockpit up the stairs and placed it on the table. Aunt Rose's laugh filled the kitchen with delight. Lilly shook my hand. "It looks so real!"

Uncle Harry looked at the cockpit, then at me, and then back to the cockpit. I could tell he was trying to think of something to say.

"It does look real," he said with a smile. "I'm just wondering how you're going to use it."

"To learn everything I need to know about aviation."

"But how?" he asked. "Who's going to teach you?"

"You are."

He laughed out loud and shook his finger at me. "You're some sleekit," he said.

CHAPTER SEVENTEEN

GROUND SCHOOL

———◦———

FOUR WEEKS HAD dragged by since I mailed my letter to Amelia Earhart. It was a waiting game, and I was not very good at waiting. In the meantime, my life had settled into a new pattern. Pat avoided me as much as she could. Sometimes she came to the store with her mom, but we just smiled at each other and exchanged a few comments. There was no need to get our families involved in our dispute.

"What's new?"

"Not much."

"Are you having company for Thanksgiving?"

"Yes."

"Us too."

In the schoolyard and after school, Pat hung around with Alice Brant and Frank Murphy. In class, our eyes rarely met. But that was fine with me. I had something to look forward to every day.

My aviation lessons with Uncle Harry had begun! He was allowing Jennie Mae to work with us, and that made everything more fun. I made sure I only stayed half an hour. I was afraid if I stayed longer, Mom might get suspicious.

We decided to stay in the basement of the hotel because Aunt Rose sometimes invited Mom for afternoon tea. She would need a map to find us in our hidden ground school. I knew we were safe.

I sat at my desk with *David Copperfield* open in front of me. But I was watching the hands on the big clock in our classroom crawl toward the twelve and the four.

Finally, the bell rang and Jennie Mae and I were free to run to the hotel. On our way through the kitchen, we said a quick hello to Lilly and Aunt Rose. The basement door was open and the light was on, which meant Uncle Harry was waiting for us. We closed the door behind us and sent up little puffs of dust as we ran down the stairs.

"Hello, girls," Uncle Harry called.

"Hello, Uncle Harry," we called back. He had given Jennie Mae permission to call him Uncle Harry, too.

"You two sit down, and I'll stand for our review." He moved to the side of the cockpit and pointed to the tachometer. "Ginny," he said.

"Tachometer," I answered. "An instrument used for indicating the rotating speed of an engine."

"Excellent," he said. "Jennie Mae." He pointed to the altimeter.

"Altimeter," Jennie Mae replied. "An instrument used for measuring the elevation of an aircraft above a given level."

"Excellent again."

The review continued until all the switches and dials on the instrument board were identified, including their function. We also went over the ten cardinal points you must know to determine your exact position when flying over the ocean: time, altitude, airspeed, groundspeed, drift, deviation, variation, whether you were using a chart or a map, true scale of miles, and magnetic compass reading.

For the last week we had been charting routes based on information Uncle Harry gave us. He said pilots needed to know how to navigate an airplane, especially when they were over water. We moved the cockpit to the floor and used the table for our maps, pencils, protractors, compasses, and rulers.

Uncle Harry unrolled a map of the North Atlantic. "Suppose you took off from a position of twenty degrees longitude and fifty degrees latitude at two in the afternoon on Tuesday," he said.

"That would be...here." I placed a heavy dot on the intersection and marked it *Point of Departure.*

"Correct. Here are the readings for your calculations." He put a piece of paper between Jennie Mae and me.

Assignment
Time: 5 P.M., Tuesday
Altitude: 10,000 feet
Airspeed Indicator Reading: 100 mph
Groundspeed: 120 mph
Drift: 10° south
Deviation: none
Variation: 15° westerly
Chart or Map: Chart
Scale of Miles: 69 miles to 1° latitude
Magnetic Compass Reading: 250°

"Now you make your calculations and explain them as you go along," Uncle Harry said.

"First we have time," Jennie Mae said. "We departed at two in the afternoon on Tuesday and it is presently five in the evening. So we know that we've been flying three hours."

"Well done," Uncle Harry said.

We worked for twenty minutes on it, but we didn't finish before it was time to go home. Uncle Harry told us to leave everything where it was so that we could finish the next day. We thanked him and hugged him goodbye.

Jennie Mae and I walked together to the store.

"I can't believe how much fun I'm having with you and Uncle Harry," she said. "Even though he knows I want to be a teacher, he still includes me in your aviation lessons."

"Uncle Harry is a good teacher," I agreed. "Maybe you can get some teaching ideas from working with him."

"You're right. I never thought of that."

For the rest of our walk, Jennie Mae was quiet. I could tell she was thinking about what I suggested. She said goodbye at the store and headed toward the farm to do her chores.

When I walked in, there were no customers. Llew had his head and arms in the apple barrel. He was removing the soft ones for Nana to make applesauce. Papa was behind the long counter, examining his account book. I took off my coat and hung it by the door just as Lilly walked in with something under her arm.

After saying hello to us, she unrolled a hooked rug on the counter. It showed the store with a man standing in the doorway wearing an apron under his suit coat. Llew joined us, and we all agreed the man looked like Papa.

"I hope you'll accept this rug as a thank-you for the burlap sacks you've given me over the last year," Lilly said.

"This beautiful rug is more than enough for those old bags," Papa said. He laid the rug behind the counter where he usually stood. "Oh, that's lovely. My old back will enjoy the softness as much as my feet will enjoy the warmth."

Lilly blushed from the compliments and then shared good news about the other rugs she made. Miss Rorke was so impressed with her work that she showed them to the other teachers. They offered her a full-time job as their housekeeper. Since the three of them shared one house, they thought it was a good arrangement for all of them.

"Maybe I could work part-time for Aunt Rose now that you're leaving," I said.

"She'll certainly need the help," Lilly replied.

I turned to Papa. "May I ask Aunt Rose, please?"

"The final decision is your mom's," he answered, "but I suppose it won't hurt to see what Rose has in mind."

I grabbed my coat off the hooks by the front door, pulled it on, and waved to Lilly, Llew, and Papa. As I hurried back to the hotel, I couldn't believe my good luck. I had a second chance to earn money for my flying lessons.

Aunt Rose was having a cup of tea at the kitchen table when I walked in. I mentioned Lilly's visit and her news about the teachers hiring her. Aunt Rose said she would be sorry to lose her because she really needed the help.

"That's why I'm here," I told her. "I'd like Lilly's job."

"That's the best news I've had all day." Aunt Rose stood up and gave me a big hug.

"Things have changed in my life and I need money for a special project, if you know what I mean."

She winked at me to show she understood. "Then this is the perfect arrangement."

She shook my hand and we sat down to talk about a work schedule. She was aware that Mom and Nana might want me to help out at home, and so she suggested two days after school and all day Saturday. I liked the idea of spending most of my time in the kitchen with her.

I announced the good news at the supper table that evening.

"Rose shouldn't be making arrangements without my permission," Mom said.

"Please." I clasped my hands under my chin. "It's only part-time."

Every eye at the table was directed at Mom. She sighed and looked at Papa. "I'll think about it."

At least she didn't say no.

CHAPTER EIGHTEEN

JOY AND TRAGEDY

———◇———

W HEN JENNIE MAE and I sat down at the table in Aunt Rose's basement for our next flying lesson, Uncle Harry pulled an envelope out of his pocket. I was afraid to breathe. I looked at Jennie Mae, whose eyes were opened wide, and then back at Uncle Harry.

"Apparently, I wrote a letter to Amelia Earhart," he said as he tapped the envelope in the palm of his hand.

"I'm so sorry I didn't tell you before it arrived," I said. "I just couldn't find the right time. Then I was afraid to tell you in case you got angry and cancelled our aviation lessons."

"We have such a good time with you," Jennie Mae added.

Uncle Harry smiled. "I guess you better see what this says."

He handed the envelope to me. It was addressed to him, and the return address simply read A. E., with a street name in Boston, Massachusetts, U.S.A. The flap had already been

89

opened. I slipped out the letter and held it so Jennie Mae could read it with me.

Dear Ginny,

Most of the letters I get ask for a picture with my signature, but yours is different. That is why I am answering it.

I'm very impressed with your current training. As a matter of fact, my first experience was with automobile mechanics, too. I'm sure your Uncle Harry can teach you how the mechanics of the plane are similar to those of a car. You can learn much from someone with his knowledge and experience.

Having people who believe in your dream is also very helpful. They will support you when your plans don't always go the way you hope they will.

As for how you feel about flying, I share your passion. As soon as I saw my first plane in the air, I knew what I wanted to do. Aside from flying myself nothing gives me more pleasure than encouraging other young women to do the same. If there are enough of us, the rest of the world might accept the idea that women make good pilots.

When I took my first flying lesson, I had the advantage of being twenty-one and having a job to pay for my lessons. I was also in a place where lessons were available.

I advise you to write to me just before you finish school. In the meantime, keep doing that valuable training with your Uncle Harry.

I wish you all the best and hope to hear from you again.

Sincerely,
Amelia Earhart

In a daze, I said, "Amelia Earhart answered my letter."

"I can't believe how lucky you are!" Jennie Mae jumped up and hugged me.

I hugged her back and then turned to Uncle Harry. "Will you teach me how the mechanics of the plane are similar to the car?"

"Do I have a choice?"

I grinned. "Not really. After all, the request is coming directly from Amelia Earhart."

Uncle Harry laughed and gave me his own big hug. "You better come to Aunt Rose's garage tomorrow after school."

"I'll be there—but right now I have to show my letter to Papa."

Uncle Harry smiled and nodded.

I folded it carefully, put it back in the envelope, and laid it between the pages of my history book so it wouldn't get wrinkled. I thanked Uncle Harry and kissed his cheek. Then Jennie Mae and I ran up the stairs and out onto Water Street.

Before she left me to head home, she grabbed my hand and squeezed it. "I still can't believe it. Amelia Earhart answered your letter."

"Wouldn't it be wonderful if I was the first aviatrix from Harbour Grace, Newfoundland!" I said. Jennie Mae was so excited she jumped up and down and clapped her hands.

We said goodbye and I opened the front door to find the store unusually quiet. Llew stepped out of the front window and put his finger to his lips. He pointed to where Papa was asleep by the stove, with his chin on his chest, his feet on Lilly's rug, and his account book open on his lap. I whispered to Llew about Amelia's letter and he shook my hand.

Then I ran to Papa. For a few seconds I wasn't sure what to do, but I decided the news was too important to let him sleep. I pulled a stool over next to his chair.

"Papa," I whispered.

He didn't move. I raised my voice slightly.

"Papa." I looked at Llew, and he walked toward us.

"Papa?" I shook his arm gently and the book slid off his lap and thudded on the floor. As if in slow motion, Papa slipped sideways off the chair.

"Papa!" I screamed. Llew grabbed his head and shoulders and lowered him gently to the floor.

"Get Doc Cron," he instructed.

I was out the door, up the hill, and in the waiting room just as Mrs. Donnelly walked out of Doc Cron's office. I pushed past her and shouted, "It's Papa!"

Doc grabbed his black bag and we ran back down the hill together.

The rest of the family had joined Llew. He was sitting on the floor with Papa's head cradled on his lap. Nana was wailing, and Mom was patting her back and talking to her.

Doc knelt down and opened his bag. He took Papa's pulse with one hand and reached for his stethoscope with the other. For what seemed like a long time, he listened to Papa's chest. Then he sat back on his heels and put his hand over his eyes.

"No!" Nana screamed and dropped down on her knees next to Llewellyn. Mom stood there with her arms at her sides and a stunned look on her face. It felt as if we were frozen in some tragic family portrait.

Mom was the first to move. She knelt beside Nana and hugged her. Nana leaned over Papa's chest and whispered in his ear, "Oh, Joe. Don't leave me. Don't leave me."

Mom tried to pull her away, but Nana grabbed Papa tightly and screamed, "No! No! No!"

The buzzing in my ears got so loud that all other sounds disappeared. I seemed to float above everyone. I could see them crying and hugging and touching Papa, but I couldn't hear them.

Then everything went black.

CHAPTER NINETEEN

FINAL GOODBYE

WHEN I AWOKE, the store and everyone in it were gone. I lay still and listened. It was dark. And quiet. No, *almost* quiet. Nearby, someone was whispering. I lifted my head and just barely heard the words.

"Don't worry, Joe," the voice said. "I'll make sure nothing bad happens to Ginny. I promise." It was Uncle Harry's voice.

I lay back down on something soft against my cheek. At eye level, I saw a thin line of light. Muffled footsteps walked away. I raised my hand and peeked out from under a kind of curtain. I was in the dining room. With the view I had of the chairs on the opposite wall, I realized that I was under the table.

I lay and listened for a few more minutes before crawling out. The blinds were pulled down and the room was lit by candles. There was a long, dark box on the table. I thought I knew what it was but wasn't sure I wanted to look inside.

Just as I made up my mind that I had to stand up, I heard voices. I scrambled back under the table and curled up.

"I laid Ginny in her bed after she fainted." It was Doc Cron's voice. "I don't understand why she isn't there."

How strange. I didn't remember being in bed.

"She may have been gone all night," Mom said. "I think we'd better call Rose and Harry."

Mom walked out, but Doc stayed next to the table. "I think Ginny will miss you most, Joe," he said. "Keep her safe for us, will you?" He walked across the carpet and down the hall.

So it was true.

Papa was dead and that was his coffin on the table above me. I curled up into a tighter ball and stuffed the cuff of my sweater into my mouth. The tears ran across my nose and into my hair.

"Ginny, are you under there?" I opened my eyes to find the line of light under the curtain was a little brighter. Someone was whispering my name. "Ginny? It's me, Uncle Harry," the voice said. "Don't worry, I won't tell them where you are. Just answer me."

"Papa is dead, Uncle Harry."

"I know, Ginny."

"I can't leave him all alone."

"Will you come out if I stay with him?"

"Maybe in a little while. How did you know where I was?"

"Llewellyn figured it out, but he wasn't comfortable coming up over the stairs into the house," he replied. "He came and told me you'd be somewhere close to your papa, and this is the only place we haven't looked."

Uncle Harry went on to tell me the funeral would be tomorrow, so this was a good time to come out. He said he would sit all night with Papa. I lifted the curtain and saw him sitting on one of the chairs against the wall. He signalled me to hurry. I crawled out and sat beside him. Just as he put his arm around my shoulders, Mom walked in.

"My God, you're back!" she said. "Where have you been?"

I pointed under the table.

For the next ten minutes, Mom yelled at me. She called me wilful, stubborn, selfish, and uncaring. Then she offered me breakfast. But I wasn't very hungry. I finished some tea and toast and went back into the dining room.

This time, I looked at Papa in his coffin. He was a bit pale but otherwise looked as if he was sleeping. I climbed up on the table and kissed his forehead the way he always kissed mine. His skin felt cool and dry. I wanted to say something to him, but I couldn't. The lump in my throat was too big. I climbed down and sat beside Uncle Harry. We didn't need to talk. It just felt safe to be there.

At ten thirty the next morning, Uncle Harry, Doc Cron, Mr. Strapp, Mr. Parsons, Mr. Whitman, and Cousin Charlie Ross carried Papa's coffin down to the funeral carriage. A black horse pulled it and the pallbearers walked beside it.

Mom and Nana wore black hats and veils. I couldn't see Nana's face, but I could hear her crying. Aunt Rose took one arm and Mom took her other one. Billy and I held hands and followed them. Behind us walked Doc Cron, Auntie Irene, and Pat.

I knew people were standing outside their stores and houses all along Water Street, but I kept my eyes on the ground and let the tears run down my face and onto my scarf. I tried not to make any noise so as not to upset Nana.

Inside the church the coffin was opened and lots of people walked by to say goodbye to Papa. Some said the actual words, but most just touched his hands.

I don't know what the minister said. My mind was remembering all the things Papa and I had done together— the regattas at Lady Lake, the picnics and fishing at Rocky Pond, blueberry picking, swimming at Bear's Cove, and working in the store. Behind my closed eyes, Papa was smiling, talking, and laughing, and I was smiling and laughing with him. For a few minutes the pain went out of my chest and I felt safe again.

Suddenly everyone stood up and started singing. The minister closed the coffin and stood over it. I couldn't breathe. My chest moved in and out, but no air came in. My fingers felt numb. My heart pounded in my ears.

Just as I felt my knees buckling, a huge gasp of air filled my lungs. No one even noticed the sound above the singing. I held onto the railing at the front of the pew and took a few more breaths.

The pallbearers moved forward and carried the coffin down the aisle. The minister followed and Nana, supported by Mom and Aunt Rose, followed him. I kept my eyes down and let the tears roll onto my scarf again. Someone took my arm, and I looked up to see Auntie Irene. She reached for Billy's hand, and then we walked out into the brisk air to see the coffin back on the carriage.

At the cemetery, the pallbearers carried Papa to a freshly dug rectangle in the ground. They put wide straps under the coffin and lowered it carefully into the hole. The minister was speaking, but the only words I heard were *ashes to ashes, dust to dust.* I knew other people were standing around us because I heard the rustle of their clothes and the sniffing or quiet crying. I jumped when a rumble of earth fell on the lid of the coffin. Others threw in handfuls and whispered goodbye to Papa before I heard them walking away.

When I raised my eyes, Aunt Rose, Uncle Harry, and I were the only ones left.

"It's time to go now, Ginny," Uncle Harry said. He put his arm around my shoulder.

"I can't leave Papa alone."

"Papa isn't in that box, Ginny," Aunt Rose said gently.

I looked up at her. "He's not?"

"I think he's probably flying around, free as a bird, watching everything that's going on down here," she said.

"Papa knows you have a big job ahead of you, Ginny, if you're going to be a pilot," Uncle Harry said.

"You have to take care of yourself, my pet," Aunt Rose added. "You have to be strong and healthy—physically and mentally—if you want your dream to come true."

"Do you really think Papa is looking at us now?" I asked.

"I'm sure of it," Uncle Harry said. "As sure as I'm standing here."

I smiled and nodded. I liked the idea that Papa was still with us.

Aunt Rose wrapped her arm around my waist, and the three of us walked down the hill to Water Street.

At the hotel, Lilly had tea and cookies laid out for our relatives. When I walked in, she put her arms around me while I cried on her shoulder. Pat and Auntie Irene told me how sorry they were, but I was too tired to talk to them. Others came and went in a blur, and then Uncle Harry offered to drive us home.

Jennie Mae and Llew stood outside the store with a small bouquet of flowers. They each gave me a hug before I stepped in the door. I kept my eyes straight ahead so I wouldn't have to look at the long counter. The inside stairs had never seemed as hard to climb as they did then.

In the kitchen, Aunt Rose put a fish pie in the oven and made tea. She and Uncle Harry led us in memories of Papa. Sometimes we laughed and sometimes we cried and it really seemed as if he was there with us.

Eventually the women did the dishes and Aunt Rose and Uncle Harry left. One by one we headed off to our rooms. When I crawled into bed, I heard Nana crying through the grate in the floor. I cried with her until I was too tired to cry any more.

PART TWO

CHAPTER TWENTY

MARCH 1932

———◄◦►———

I T HAD BEEN five months since the funeral, but the ache in my chest started as soon as I opened the front door. In my head I knew Papa wasn't there, but my eyes and ears and heart still expected him to be sitting by the stove or standing behind the long counter.

I closed the door and looked around. The upper shelves were bare, and Dad was arranging the tins on the lower shelves to fill in the empty spaces. He couldn't get home from Toronto in time for the funeral but had arrived the following week. He had been trying to run the store even though Bowring Brothers hadn't sent a shipment since I got the reward for finding Tailwind.

I wiped my galoshes on the mat and started to take off my coat when the cold hit me. I quickly pulled it back over my shoulders and walked to the stove. A few coals glowed in the bottom.

"We're saving the coal for upstairs," Dad said.

I nodded in agreement just as Llew emerged through the trap door from the basement and handed Dad a big cloth bag of flour.

"Oh... hi, Gin," he said.

Before I could answer, he turned to Dad. "This is the last of the supplies, Mr. Ross."

"At least they're the staples that people still need," Dad pointed out. Then he turned to me. "You better ask your mom what she needs for upstairs before I put this lot out on the shelves," he said. "She won't want to be buying it elsewhere when we run out."

I didn't say a word, but we all knew there was little money to buy anything once we ran out. Llew was right. He said we would feel the Depression more in the spring when the fishers, sealers, and whalers weren't getting paid. If they had no money, they couldn't pay us.

As if he just read my mind, Robert McFarlane walked in the front door with four nice trout on a string. "Caught them through the ice on Rocky Pond," he told us. He took off his cap before he continued. "Your father, God rest his soul, always gave us what we needed whether we had money or not. I'll put them against my bill, if you don't mind, Mr. Ross."

"Not at all, my boy," Dad replied. "Nana will appreciate these."

It wasn't so long ago Nana bristled at the idea of fish, rabbits, and vegetables instead of money. But since Papa died she just ate whatever Mom put in front of her. Dad handed me the fish and I walked up the inside stairs.

I felt the warmth of the kitchen just standing in the doorway. Nana sat in her rocker, her hands folded in her lap. Mom chopped potatoes and carrots at one end of the table and Billy played with his toy soldiers at the other end.

Mom looked up. "Look at these beauties, Nana." She stood up and took the fish from me. "We'll have these for our supper," she said, before she dropped them into the sink.

I gave her Dad's message about the staples and she headed downstairs. I slipped off my hat and coat and pulled a chair in front of Nana's rocker. I only had a few minutes to talk to her because I now worked at the hotel every day after school and all day on Saturday. Mom gave me permission to accept Aunt Rose's offer after Papa died. In fact, I was working more hours than Aunt Rose thought Mom would allow.

I took Nana's hand in both of mine. "How are you?"

She looked at me but said nothing.

"Mom said she's been sitting there all day," Billy told me.

"Did you have some lunch?" I asked Nana.

"Mom said she hasn't eaten all day," Billy answered again.

"It's time for me to go to Aunt Rose's, Nana. You eat some dinner and I'll bring you dessert from the hotel."

She took my face in her hands and kissed my forehead like Papa used to do. I felt tears building up.

I told her I would get my supper at Aunt Rose's. With my outside clothes under my arm, I ran up to my bedroom to get Amelia's letter. Just touching it made me feel better. I slipped it out of the envelope and tucked it in my pocket.

At the Archibald Hotel, light shone through the downstairs windows onto the snow. I climbed the front steps, opened the door, and followed the voices to the kitchen, where Aunt Rose and Uncle Harry were just starting their supper.

"There's more fish chowder in the pot, Ginny," Aunt Rose said. "Dig in."

"This will cure all that ails you," Uncle Harry added.

After one bowl with bread and butter, I felt better. The cold slowly left my body and the pain in my chest eased. A slice of apple pie with tea and I was more like my old self.

"Before you get too comfortable, my pet," Aunt Rose said, "you have soup to make for tomorrow while I keep an eye on the customers in the beverage room." She opened her cookbook to a recipe for cream of potato soup and reminded me to wash the dishes and the floor before I had my tea break.

While I worked my way through the recipe, Uncle Harry kept me company, reading one of his aviation books.

"What are you going to teach me next?" I asked.

"Let's see. You can service a car and apply that knowledge to a plane. You can plot a route, even over water. You can identify the function of the instruments on the instrument board. Aside from actually flying a plane, what's left?"

"Maybe we could go over the steps I should take from the time I get in a plane until I'm in the air."

"I better review them myself," he said as he ran his finger down the index.

Although I worked in the kitchen, I had a lot to learn. I pointed to the recipe and asked Uncle Harry what *scald the milk* meant. He said I should heat it without bringing it to a boil. He flipped through a few more pages in his book and then looked up at me.

"I think I'll have a sandwich for lunch tomorrow," he said.

"Thanks a lot," I replied. "I'm underwhelmed by your confidence in my cooking."

We were both laughing when Aunt Rose walked back into the kitchen. She sat down and asked me to make her a cup of tea. Uncle Harry described my lack of cooking skills and her hearty laugh filled the kitchen.

When her sitting time was up, she told me Dad was in the beverage room. She would take him a bowl of soup with bread and butter and he could walk home with me.

I nodded in agreement. I knew Dad wouldn't disagree with anything Aunt Rose said. As a matter of fact, no one disagreed with anything Aunt Rose said—or did.

On the one hand, it had been good to have Dad home. He minded the store when Mom was upstairs taking care of Nana, cooking, or cleaning. On the other hand, it hadn't been so good because he and Mom argued constantly about all the time and money he spent drinking beer at the hotel. Any time a bit of money came into the store, he was right there to pocket it.

When he finished his supper, Dad and I put on our outside clothes and headed home. We walked in silence. It was hard to believe the world could be so beautiful without Papa in it. The night sky was clear and the stars seemed near enough to touch. The snow crunched under our boots and my nostrils stuck together when I took a deep breath.

"I miss Papa."

Dad took my hand. "I do, too, Ginny. I do, too."

We continued in silence, lost in our own thoughts.

The store was dark by the time Dad and I walked in. He told me to go upstairs while he added a bit more coal to the stove to prevent what was left of the produce from freezing.

Mom and Nana sat at the kitchen table talking quietly. Mom patted Nana's hand, but she just stared into the distance.

"Oh, it's you." Mom looked toward the doorway. "Make yourself some tea and toast, and off you go to bed." She helped Nana up and supported her as they left the kitchen.

While the kettle boiled I took Amelia's letter out of my pocket and read it again. The kettle whistled and I got up from the table to make the tea and slice the bread for the toast rack.

"What's this?"

I dropped the knife and turned around to see Mom standing at the table with Amelia's letter in her hand. I was too surprised to answer.

"I told you there would be no more talk about planes in

this house—and now it's a pilot you want to be!" She ripped the letter in half.

I lunged toward her, but a powerful slap across my face stopped me. I put my hand on my cheek and blinked to regain my focus.

In those few seconds, she threw the letter into the stove and swung around to face me again. Tears filled her eyes. "I'll tell you what you're going to be," she said. "Out to work full-time to help me hold this family together."

I felt my own eyes filling up with tears, but I'd be damned if I cried. "If you think I'm quitting school, you're crazy!"

"You'll do as you're told, missy, or suffer the consequences." Her pointed finger punctuated every word. She swiped her arm across her eyes and stormed out of the kitchen.

I slumped down on one of the chairs and let the tears flow. Amelia said I had to finish school before I took flying lessons. Mom was going to spoil all my plans.

But she wasn't going to succeed. I wouldn't let that happen.

CHAPTER TWENTY-ONE

FINDING AMELIA

——◄o►——

BEFORE ANYONE WAS up, I slipped downstairs and prepared some provisions—two blueberry jam sandwiches, some oatmeal cookies, and a handful of raisins. With everything wrapped in brown paper, I carefully placed the food with the extra clothes in my school bag. Just as I left the kitchen, Nana walked out of her bedroom at the end of the hall.

"Morning, Nana."

She smiled and moved slowly toward the kitchen as I went up to my bedroom. I opened the drapes and looked out onto the vast whiteness of the frozen bay. The only ships were in Munn's dry dock at Point O' Beach. To put in time before breakfast, I made my bed and hung up yesterday's clothes. The last thing I added to my school bag was *David Copperfield*, which I slipped down the side so as not to squish the sandwiches. When the grandfather clock in the parlour struck seven, I headed downstairs.

Mom, Dad, and Billy had joined Nana in the kitchen, but you wouldn't know it if you were standing in the hall outside the door. The only sounds were the occasional crunches of toast and slurps of tea from Billy.

I sat down and Mom looked up at me. "I'll call your teacher and tell her you're leaving school at the end of the week," she said.

"But I'll only have part of grade eight."

"That's all you need to continue working in the hotel," she replied.

When I looked around the table for support, Dad dropped his eyes to his plate. His hair and the bristles on his face looked longer than usual. His hand shook when he lifted his cup to his mouth. Nana licked blueberry jam off her knife and then put it back in the jar. Billy mumbled a conversation between two of his toy soldiers. I finished my toast and tea, retrieved my school bag from the inside stairs, and left the silence behind.

At school I wandered to my desk and opened *David Copperfield*. With my chin in my hand, I closed my eyes and in my mind composed my second letter to Amelia Earhart.

Dear Miss Earhart,

Since I last wrote to you, my life has changed. My papa is dead. One minute he was sitting in his chair beside the stove, and the next minute he was gone. On top of that, Mom ripped up the letter you wrote me.

She told me I have to quit school and get a full-time job to help support the family.

I can't give up my dream now, so I'm coming to see you in Boston. I'll take the train to Port aux Basques and the ferry to Nova Scotia. When I get there I'll find out how to get to Boston. But don't worry about me. Mom and Pop Davis, my other grandparents, live there and I can stay with them. I'll finish school in Boston and still be ready to take flying lessons.

I hope this is all right with you because I can't wait for a reply to this letter.

Your friend,
Ginny Ross

At recess Llew leaned against the schoolyard fence talking to his friend, Oliver Watts. I told him I wanted to speak to Llew alone. Oliver winked at me and walked away.

I turned to face Llew and whispered, "I need to borrow some money."

"How much?"

"What can you spare?"

"I have seven dollars left from the reward money my mom gave back to me," he replied.

"That would be a big help."

Llew asked why I needed the money, but I told him it was a secret. I knew he could never lie to Dad, Mom, or Nana if he knew where I was. He didn't press me for more details and agreed to bring the money to school after lunch.

I looked around the schoolyard and saw Jennie Mae talking to her sister. I wished I could tell her I was going away, but this was a secret I couldn't share with anyone.

At lunch the kitchen was quiet again. I had nothing to say to Mom, and Nana seemed to be off somewhere else. Maybe she was thinking of her life before Papa died. Every now and then she smiled or hummed to herself.

When Mom started washing the dishes, I slipped an envelope out of the drawer in the kitchen table and walked up to my room. I sat at my desk and quickly wrote the letter. Thank goodness Mom hadn't found Amelia's envelope. I took it off the shelf in my wardrobe and copied her address and Uncle Harry's return address. On my way back to school, I dropped my letter off at the post office.

"This is your Uncle Harry's second letter to Amelia Earhart," the postmaster said. "I guess he's interested in pilots these days."

"He sure is!" I smiled and turned away from the counter, in case he wanted to talk more about "Uncle Harry's" letter.

I paid for the stamp and walked back to school.

Llew was standing at the school gate. When I reached him, he slipped some folded bills into my hand. "Mind you, don't let Nana know where you got this."

I smiled and nodded. So that was it. He thought the money was to help Nana. The bell rang and we walked into line together. The grade tens moved inside before my class. Llew looked back and gave me a thumbs-up. I returned it, but I felt the heat of shame climbing up my face.

The afternoon dragged on until the final bell. Everyone raced down the stairs and out to the schoolyard. I felt a lump in my throat when I waved to Jennie Mae and Llew. They waved back and headed in opposite directions—one to the farm and the other to the store. I waited until they were both out of sight and then walked quickly along Harvey Street to the train station.

Mr. Whitman, the ticket agent, smiled when I walked in. "What would Miss Ginny like today?"

That was the problem with being a store owner's granddaughter. Everyone in town knew me.

"A ticket to Port aux Basques," I replied.

"That's a long time on the train," he said. "What's taking you there?"

I didn't have an answer ready, so a few seconds ticked by. "I'm visiting a friend."

"What about school?"

"I'm ahead of the others, so Miss Rorke, my teacher, said a few days off won't hurt."

"That will cost you ten shillings each way."

I explained I only had American money from my reward for finding Tailwind. What I didn't tell him was that I took it from the chocolate tin in Mom's bedroom to add to Llew's money.

Mr. Whitman said he could convert the dollars to shillings. He had to do it for Mr. Brown and then Mr. Mears when they left town.

I could have saved money by purchasing a one-way ticket like they did, but that would have told Mr. Whitman I wasn't coming back.

CHAPTER TWENTY-TWO

THE TRAIN

———◄○►———

T HE WAITING ROOM was empty, so I sat in the corner farthest from the door. The next half-hour was agony. The image of Llew's trusting face was locked in my mind. Maybe I could write him a letter from Boston to apologize for not being honest. This solution should have eased my anxiety, but it didn't. I was afraid someone I knew would walk in and ask where I was going.

At last the train approached, bell ringing and wheels screeching. I waited until it stopped completely and then ran out the door next to the tracks. The conductor took my arm and helped me up the steps.

I found a seat by the window away from the platform and sank into the red velvet upholstery. Warm air touched my face, so I took off my hat, coat, and mitts. I slouched to hide from anyone waving goodbye at the train.

At Whitbourne, the door at the end of my car opened and a woman about Mom's age walked in.

"The car next door is full of fishermen," she said. "They're a lovely lot, but they'll sing and smoke all the way to Port aux Basques." She smiled and twisted the handle on her purse. "Do you mind if I join you?"

I smiled back. "Not at all."

She put a small suitcase on the rack above the seat and sat opposite me. She wore a long black coat, black lace-up boots, a black hat with a veil folded over the top, and a black purse and gloves. Even her hair was black.

A blast of steam, the ringing of the bell, and the train lurched forward. *Chunk, chunk, chunk.* Slowly the movement got smoother as the train picked up speed and the tracks began to clickety-clack.

"Where are you going?" the woman asked as she took off her hat and laid it on the seat next to her.

"Ah…to see my grandparents in Boston."

"Such a long trip for a young lady."

"Mom Davis, my grandmother, is sick, and she wants to see me."

"It's good you're taking the time to do that."

"Where are you going?" I asked.

"I live in Port aux Basques, but I was in St. John's for the reading of my husband's will."

"Oh, I'm sorry," I said.

Her eyes filled with tears. She looked out the window and smoothed her dress over her knees. I waited a few minutes before I asked another question. "Do you have any children?"

She dabbed her eyes with a lace hanky and looked over at me. "We were never blessed that way," she said. "But I have a job at the local pharmacy to keep me busy."

I couldn't think of anything else to say, and so the conversation ended. We both looked out the window at the black trees etched against the white snow. The sky was darkening quickly. The woman looked at her watch. "I guess I'll head into the dining car. Are you ready for some supper?"

"I brought sandwiches, thank you," I told her.

"By the way, I'm Elizabeth Harris." She leaned over with her hand outstretched, and I shook it.

"I'm Virginia Ross, but everyone calls me Ginny."

"It's a pleasure to meet you, Ginny."

With the car to myself again, I sank back into the plush seat. Leaving home was my only option if I wanted to become a pilot. But now that I was on my way, I had a funny feeling in my stomach. It was hard to explain, except to say I was on guard all the time, waiting for something to go wrong.

I took out *David Copperfield.* Reading made me feel calmer—and hungry. I ate one sandwich, one cookie, and a few raisins. I would have loved a cup of tea, but saving my money was more important. The ferry to Nova Scotia and the train to Boston would probably be expensive.

With Charles Dickens as my guide, I continued through David Copperfield's life. When my eyes got tired, I lay down, covered myself with my coat, and closed my eyes. My mind wandered back to the store. I sat in the warmth of the stove with my book opened on my lap. Papa stood behind the long counter with his inventory book in front of him.

"Ginny?" he said, but his mouth wasn't moving. "Ginny?" he repeated, but again his mouth remained closed in a smile.

I opened my eyes, and in the dim light of the train I saw a familiar outline sitting across from me.

"Is that you, Papa?" I sat up and pulled my coat under my chin.

"Who else would know you're going to Boston to see Amelia Earhart?"

"How do you know that?"

"I know everything."

"Are you alive, Papa?"

"No, Ginny." I could see his sad smile even in the dim light.

"Are you a ghost?"

"More like a spirit who can see all the people he loves."

I felt safe and warm sitting with Papa. Then I thought of everything I'd done to get there. The warmth disappeared.

"I left them alone." I looked away so he couldn't see the tears in my eyes—but I turned back quickly in case he disappeared. "Was I wrong to do that?" I wrapped my arms around my legs and rested my chin on my knees.

"Why don't you think about it for a while, Ginny?" Papa stood up and turned toward the aisle.

"Don't leave me." I reached for his hand and he turned to face me.

"I'll be back, Ginny. You'll never be alone." With that, he walked up the aisle, waved once, and disappeared.

I lay down again and pulled my coat up to my chin. Aunt Rose and Uncle Harry were right. Papa wasn't in that coffin in the ground; he was flying around and watching over us. I closed my eyes and let the feeling of warmth surround me again.

CHAPTER TWENTY-THREE

STUCK

———◦———

W HEN I WOKE, I couldn't remember where I was. I lay
still until the motion of the train reminded me I
was on my way to Boston. I turned my head and looked
around. Elizabeth Harris was asleep with her head resting
on the back of the seat. I checked the pocket in my dress to
make sure my money was still there. Not that I didn't trust
Elizabeth. It was part of the feeling I had that something
would go wrong before I got to Boston.

Quietly, I got up and walked in the direction Elizabeth
had gone last night. The swaying train bounced me from
one side of the aisle to the other. Where the cars were
coupled together, a platform exposed the swirling snow on
the tracks. I was afraid to step on it, but I knew I had to.
A giant leap and one foot barely touched the steel square
before I was on the other side.

The dining car was straight ahead, beyond a glass door. A
man was already sitting at a small table covered by a white

tablecloth and silver cutlery. A waiter wearing a short white coat handed him a menu and then opened the door for me.

"Table, miss?"

I leaned over and whispered, "Where's the bathroom?"

With a smile he pointed to the opposite end of the dining car.

When I returned, the waiter walked up to me again, and I told him I just wanted a cup of tea. He seated me at a table and returned a few minutes later with a big pot of tea and some milk and sugar. I smiled and thanked him. A whole pot of tea! I could have at least two cups and then my blueberry jam sandwich back in the compartment. I poured my first cup and savoured the sweet warmth.

The door opened again and the fishermen piled in. They sat together at two of the tables. One of them had an accordion, and as soon as their tea was ordered, he began to play.

"Lots of fish in Bonavist' Harbour, lots of fish..." they sang, and I joined them. They called me a bonnie lass and we sang a few more songs. With the arrival of their tea, our concert ended. In the silence I drank my tea and watched the moving curtain of snow that blew past the window.

"May I join you?" Elizabeth Harris brought my attention back to the table.

"Please do," I replied.

No sooner had she sat down than the brakes screeched and the train slowed to a stop.

"Waiter?" Elizabeth raised her hand. "What's happening?"

"It must be a snowdrift, missus, blocking the tracks," he explained. "We'll be at Gaff Topsails. We always get stuck here in the winter."

I wanted to get to Port aux Basques before anyone at home figured out where I was heading.

"How long will we be here?" I asked the waiter.

"Till the plow can get through to us, miss."

I groaned inwardly. Knowing my luck, Mom or Uncle Harry would be riding on the snowplow right now. They would take me off the train and back to Harbour Grace before I got to Boston to find Amelia.

"I remembers de time she got stuck in for five days," one of the fishermen said.

"Well, I gots plenty o' grub wid me," said another.

People around us laughed and the stories continued until a short man with large black glasses walked into the car and someone shouted, "'Tis de union fella!"

I looked at Elizabeth and she told me it was Joey Smallwood, who had been organizing the fishermen to form a union. He'd been going all over Newfoundland giving speeches. She thought he might be running for government, too.

People reached out to shake his hand. He stopped and chatted with each one before he sat down at a table with the fishermen.

"So Joey, when are we gonna see de end o' dis Depression?" an old man asked him.

"Let me wet my whistle with a bit of tea before I get talking."

We laughed again and one of the men at the table poured him a cup of tea. Joey made a slurping sound. "That's some good, that is," he said.

He ordered toast and then turned back to the man who asked the question.

"Well, Skipper, it's like this. No one really knows. The banks will take time to get back on their feet and, until that happens, there's no money circulating."

"My whole family is fishermen and sealers and der's no money from de fish or seals," a younger man said.

"Nor de whales," an old man said and raised the pipe in his hand.

"I wants ta fish, Joey, but I gots to go to Corner Brook to cut wood for de pulp and paper," another young man said.

"Yes, b'y, it's the same everywhere," Joey replied. "That's why we need a fishermen's union. To get rid of those pirates on Water Street!"

The fishermen cheered and patted Joey on the back. "Here's what we need to do...."

I looked out the window at the wind blowing the snow higher and higher up the glass. The conversation was quieter now since people chatted with those sitting close to them. Elizabeth was turned in her seat talking to the man behind her. I wondered if the Depression had something to do with Papa's death. Doc Cron said it was a heart attack. Maybe worrying about no money coming in caused it.

I excused myself and walked back to the compartment, which was much easier to do with the train stopped. I flopped into my seat and wrote on the ice in the corner of the window, *A.E. 1932.* I hoped to see her, but I had no idea what lay ahead.

Just as I adjusted the curtain so my printing couldn't be seen, Elizabeth sat back in her seat. I looked at her black clothes and remembered what she had said about her husband's will.

"Do you believe in ghosts?" I asked.

She surprised me by answering immediately. "Yes, I do."

"Have you ever seen one?"

"Right after my husband died, I saw him sitting in his favourite chair in the parlour. We talked for quite a while. He seems to show up when I'm sad or frightened or worried."

"I saw my grandfather sitting right where you are now."

She smiled and said she hoped she wasn't squishing him. I told her not to worry because he left last night.

I felt sad, frightened, and worried—sad because Papa died, frightened I wouldn't be able to find Amelia, and worried about the people at home. I didn't want to think about anything except getting to Boston, but I kept seeing my family's faces before I left. Papa was right. I had a lot of thinking to do.

CHAPTER TWENTY-FOUR

DECISION

◄○►

"THE FERRY TO North Sydney, Nova Scotia, doesn't run every day," Elizabeth said. "You can stay at my house if you need to wait for it."

"Ah... that's very kind of you." This was not good news. I was hoping there wouldn't be any more delays.

"I know you're anxious to see your grandmother. You may be lucky enough to have the ferry sailing the same day we arrive in Port aux Basques."

I smiled at Elizabeth. "I'll keep my fingers crossed."

We looked out the window for a few minutes and then picked up our books at the same time. I wasn't really reading, though. I was thinking about all the lying I was doing. Elizabeth wanted to help me, and I thanked her by telling her one lie after another. I looked over at her and cleared my throat. She looked up, but I didn't know where to start.

"I have a confession."

"Oh?"

"I'm not going to see my grandparents. I mean, I am going to stay with them, but they're not the real reason I'm going to Boston. I'm going there to find Amelia Earhart."

Elizabeth's eyes widened. "Why would you want to do that?"

"I want to be a pilot just like her, and I need to find out where and how to get flying lessons."

"I see."

Elizabeth asked about missing school and about my family. This time I told the truth about Papa's death, Dad's time at the hotel, Mom's insistence that I quit school and go to work, and Nana's behaviour, including how she wasn't eating or sleeping.

Elizabeth shook her head and whispered, "How sad for all of you."

I shrugged my shoulders as if to say *what can we do?* The lump in my throat stopped me from speaking.

She leaned over and took my hand in both of hers. When she saw the tears in my eyes, she quietly sat with me and patted my hand.

After many minutes, she asked, "How about a cup of tea?"

"I think I'll just stay here," I replied. "I have some thinking to do."

"Then I'll leave you for a while." She squeezed my hand and smiled before she left.

Just as I leaned my head on the back of the seat and

pulled my coat over my legs, Elizabeth opened the door to the dining car. I heard faint accordion music and a chorus of "I'se the B'y."

I closed my eyes and heard "I'se the B'y" again, but this time I saw the store decorated in evergreen boughs for Christmas. The mummers sang and all our neighbours joined in. A big mummer in his wife's clothes danced Papa around the stove while Uncle Harry laughed and clapped. Mom talked with Aunt Rose, and while Nana arranged the food on the long counter, Dad poured whisky from behind the short one. Billy sat on the inside stairs stuffing his mouth with chocolates.

Suddenly the lights in the store dimmed and the crowd disappeared. In my mind, I floated upstairs into a grey silence. I found them in the kitchen, sitting just as I had left them. No one was eating, no one was drinking, and no one was talking, not even Billy.

Dad stood up and walked down the inside stairs. Mom followed him, and I floated down after them. She stopped in the middle of the store and shouted to Dad. "Don't leave me alone again with that crazy mother of yours." He opened the front door and walked out. Mom put her hands over her face and her shoulders shook. Then I heard the saddest sound I'd ever heard.

"Do I go on or do I go back home?" I whispered. For what seemed like hours, I tossed and turned.

When I opened my eyes, Papa was sitting across from

me in Elizabeth's seat. I sat up and faced him. "I've made my decision."

He smiled. "Tell me about it."

"I'm going on to Boston. I have to find Amelia Earhart and finish my education. Look at what happened when Dad came home from Toronto. Nothing changed. The family is still in trouble. If I become a pilot, I not only help myself but also them. I could make enough money to support the whole family. In the meantime, I know Aunt Rose and Uncle Harry will make sure they're okay. They may even take them to the hotel to live until these hard times are over."

I brushed away the tears that ran down my face. "I have to be the strong one, Papa. I'm the only one who can change my life and theirs."

He nodded. "I know it has been a tough decision, Ginny, and I'm proud of you."

Once again he stood up and walked down the aisle. He stopped at the door between the cars, blew me a kiss, and then faded away. But this time I didn't feel alone. I knew he would always be with me.

I snuggled under my coat again and pictured Mom, Nana, Dad, Billy, and Uncle Harry sitting in the kitchen at the hotel. The room was warm and well-lit. There were big bowls of pea soup with bread, butter, tea, and molasses buns on the table. Aunt Rose entertained them with another impression of Doc Cron and they laughed and clapped their hands.

CHAPTER TWENTY-FIVE

PORT AUX BASQUES

—◄◦►—

ELIZABETH RETURNED FROM the dining car and sat beside me. She took my hand in both of hers again. "Feeling better?" she asked.

"Much better, thanks."

"Come and have a hot meal with me."

I only had a few raisins left from home, so a hot meal sounded wonderful. But now that I was definitely going to Boston, I had to watch every penny. Anyway, it wouldn't hurt me to skip a few meals.

"I need to save my money for the rest of my trip," I said.

"That's why I invited you," Elizabeth said. "Dinner is on me."

"In that case, I'd be delighted!"

I followed her into the dining car, where the singing and laughing continued. The fishermen were still sharing the food they brought from home, but it took many pots of tea to wash it all down.

Over dinner, I mentioned her offer to have me stay at her house until the ferry sailed. I apologized for hesitating when she first mentioned it but explained that I was anxious to get to Boston.

"I'm delighted, Ginny. I wasn't looking forward to going home alone. The dark, cold house would only remind me that Walter is gone."

"You'll be helping me finish my great adventure," I said.

She laughed. "You've already had a great adventure. Most girls your age haven't been outside the towns they were born in."

We finished our baked cod and winter vegetables and returned to our seats. Elizabeth offered me five pounds for the trip to Boston. I hesitated, knowing about Llewellyn's money, but she said she wouldn't feel easy unless I took it.

"Just think—I'll be able to tell people I helped Ginny Ross, the famous aviatrix," she said.

I thanked her and tucked the money into my pocket.

I tried to read, but the hot meal and the warmth of the train were too much for my concentration. My head dropped forward and then snapped upright as I fought the sleepy feeling that came over me.

Elizabeth put her book aside and turned off the overhead light. I curled up. The last thing I remembered was snuggling under my coat while a soft hand stroked my head.

A voice woke me. "Did you feel that?" It was Elizabeth.

The train jerked forward.

"You mean that?" I asked.

Just then the door to our car opened and the conductor ran in.

"The plow is here!" He continued through to the next car with the same announcement. Soon the jerks were followed by solid *chunk, chunk, chunks*, and the train moved again. The swaying and the clickety-clacking of the wheels were hypnotic. In spite of my excitement, sleep came easily.

———◁◎▷———

"Port aux Basques, one hour!" the conductor announced as he walked down the aisle. "Tea only this morning. Tea only."

I opened my eyes to a sunny day and snow as far as I could see. Elizabeth combed her hair in the mirror over her seat before we left for the dining car. It felt good to be bouncing from one side of the aisle to the other again.

The sound of laughing and bantering back and forth greeted us when we opened the door.

"Sure, this must be the fastest winter trip this old engine ever made," the conductor said.

"Even with waiting for the plow?" Elizabeth asked.

"Even with!" he replied.

"A record time is what it is," Joey Smallwood added.

We lingered over our tea until the train pulled into the station. We all shook hands and wished each other well.

The fishermen doffed their caps to Elizabeth and me as they took our hands. Joey kissed our hands and the fishermen hooted and called him a right dandy.

Elizabeth went back to our car to get her suitcase and I waited for her by the door through which everyone was leaving. I already had my school bag with me. When she returned, the conductor helped each of us down to the platform. A cold wind swirled around us and Elizabeth grabbed her black hat just as it flew off her head. She tucked it under her arm and picked up her suitcase again.

We only walked a few steps when a man in a rough wool jacket came up to us. He took off his cap with a slight bow. "Taxi, Mrs. Harris?" he asked.

"Hello, Jake. How did you know I'd be on this train?"

"I meets all de trains what comes in, in case sommun needs a ride."

"I presume the ferry isn't running," she said.

"She haven't been runnin' all week wid de wind we had."

"In that case, I'd love a ride, Jake."

He put our bags in the front seat and we climbed in the back. Within five minutes we pulled up in front of a beautiful three-storey brick house. Jake held the car door as we got out. Then he took off his cap again.

"Would you be wantin' the fire lit in the wood stove, Mrs. Harris? Just to take off de damp?"

"That would be a great help," Elizabeth said. "Thank you."

He grabbed our bags and followed us into the house.

While she and Jake got the kitchen organized, Elizabeth invited me to look around the house. The parlour was much like ours at home: a large red oriental rug in the middle of the floor, a glass chandelier hanging over it, lace curtains in the windows, and a big mirror over the fireplace. Red velvet chairs sat on either side of the fireplace and a matching sofa faced it. All the side tables in the parlour and the dining room furniture in the adjoining room were made of heavy dark wood.

When I returned to the kitchen, a fire was roaring in the stove and the kettle was boiling. "Just tinned soup, crackers, and tea for supper," Elizabeth said.

"That's more than we need," I said. "And who knows what tomorrow will bring!"

CHAPTER TWENTY-SIX

ELIZABETH

———◆◇◆———

THE NEXT MORNING the wind was still blowing and a snowy rain was falling. Elizabeth stepped back from the kitchen window and announced what I already knew: there would be no ferry that day. Still, she wanted to walk down to the wharf to ask the ferry agent about future weather reports. After a cup of hot tea, we bundled up and headed out the door. The wind whipped our faces so hard we could barely keep our eyes opened. But we lowered our heads and trudged forward. At the wharf, the sea was the colour of lead. Whitecaps chased each other to shore in angry curls.

At least the ticket office was warm and dry. We stomped the snow off our boots and shook out our wet coats, hats, and scarves. "Any break in this weather, Charlie?" Elizabeth asked.

"No chance, Mrs. Harris," he replied. "Not for the next few days."

"We'll come back then, but if there is any change in the meantime, please let us know."

"Right you are, Mrs. Harris."

Before bundling up again we warmed our hands over the pot-bellied stove. Elizabeth turned to look at me. "I've been thinking about something, Ginny. We should send a telegram to your parents saying that you're safe."

"No, you can't. They'll come and get me, especially if the ferry can't get away."

"But look what happened to us. It could take them six days to get here on the train."

"I'd feel better if you sent a letter instead. Tell them I'm fine and you'll keep me here until the weather improves— which is the truth."

Elizabeth didn't answer.

"Please, you have to give me time to get to Boston."

Elizabeth said she would think about it but that in the meantime we had to get groceries. She asked what I liked to eat, and I told her everything. She laughed, and together we made a shopping list. Neither of us was looking forward to going back into the storm, but we knew it had to be done.

Since conversation was impossible in that gale, we walked in silence. In the grocery store we chatted as we picked out what we needed, but we returned to the house as fast as we could. Once inside we hung up our wet clothes and dashed into the kitchen to hold our hands over the wood stove again. It took some minutes before we could comfortably straighten our fingers.

"Time to get to work, my girl," Elizabeth said. "We'll have a cooked supper by this afternoon."

I had never cooked much before, aside from a few dishes at Aunt Rose's hotel, but Elizabeth got me involved right away. While I peeled the carrots, turnips, parsnips, and potatoes, Elizabeth cut the cabbage into quarters and rinsed the salt beef. She put the beef in a pot full of water and set it on the stove to boil.

When the preparations were done, we sat down at the kitchen table with a big pot of tea and made baloney sandwiches. During the rest of the morning, Elizabeth occasionally changed the water on the salt beef and we played gin rummy.

In the afternoon some of her neighbours arrived.

"Welcome back, Elizabeth," the women shouted as they came through the door. One had a pot of fish chowder, another had a loaf of fresh bread, and the third brought a plate of oatmeal cookies. "We knew you'd be tired after your trip to St. John's, so here we are." They took off their hats and coats and joined us at the table.

"And who might this be," the chowder lady asked.

"I'm Ginny Ross from Harbour Grace."

"Pleased to meet you," they all said.

I shook hands with Edwina, Ann, and Maude.

"Ginny is going to Boston to meet Amelia Earhart," Elizabeth explained. "She wants to become a pilot, just like Amelia."

"Well, you're some brave, my ducky," Maude said. "You wouldn't catch me up in one of those things for all the money in the world."

"But I must say I wouldn't mind looking like that Amelia Earhart," Ann added.

"She's some pretty, so she is," Edwina agreed.

Elizabeth set bowls of chowder on the table with the fresh bread and another big pot of tea. I couldn't believe I was sitting here talking to women about my dream without having to defend myself. No one said I was crazy, no one said I couldn't do it, and no one said planes were for men. In that kitchen I was accepted for who I was and what I wanted to be. When grateful tears built up in my eyes, I got up and poured more boiling water into the teapot.

Elizabeth's neighbours talked about her husband, Walter. He was the bank manager in town and twenty years older than her. Everyone had a story to share. Sometimes they laughed and sometimes they cried, just as we did when we came home from Papa's funeral.

After many pots full of tea and the plate of cookies were finished, the ladies announced it was time they got home. While Elizabeth walked them to the door, I started clearing the table. I thought about Papa again and knew he was watching over me. But lately someone else had been creeping into my mind. I didn't expect to miss Llew, but I often saw his smiling face and that long hair he used to push out of his eyes. After Papa died, he did take care of me. Maybe that's what I missed about him.

"I think it's time we put those vegetables into the pot," Elizabeth said as she returned to the kitchen. She showed me how to spoon them in without splashing boiling water onto myself. I didn't know learning to cook could be such fun.

An hour later we tucked into the best dinner I'd ever tasted. We didn't speak until our plates were half-empty. I thought back to the fun we had talking about Walter this afternoon. I felt I knew him because of the memories the women shared with me. I wanted Elizabeth to know Papa in the same way.

"Walter reminds me of Papa."

Elizabeth looked up from her plate. "In what way?"

"It seems as if he took care of you the same way Papa took care of me."

I told Elizabeth about how he stood up for me, especially when Mom put me down, about how he carried me all the way up to Doc Cron's and back home when I fell out of Mr. Mears's plane, about all the things we did together, and about how I used to help him by climbing up the ladder in the store. But most of all I told her he was the only one in the house who truly loved me.

"You must miss him terribly," Elizabeth said.

"I do miss him. But I'm lucky to still have Llew. He's two years older than me and has worked in the store since he was ten. He's my best friend in the same way Papa was. I can tell him anything, and I know he'll keep it to himself."

"Does Llew love you like Papa did?" she asked.

I felt my face getting hot. "Of course not! He's just a friend."

Elizabeth didn't say anything else. She just smiled and started clearing the table. When her hand moved toward me, I automatically ducked. She sat down again with a shocked look on her face.

"You thought I was going to hit you."

I looked down at my hands. I didn't know why, but I felt embarrassed about ducking.

"Does someone hit you?"

I kept my head down. "Mom," I mumbled.

"Why does she do that?"

"Sometimes I disobey her and sometimes I answer back."

"Does anyone else hit you?"

"No."

Elizabeth leaned over and hugged me. "Don't you worry," she said. "No one will hit you while I'm around!"

I hugged her back. It felt good to have someone's arms around me again.

Later that night, when we were sitting at the table reading, Elizabeth agreed to write the letter to Mom and Dad. She insisted I take another five pounds to get me to

Boston. She also insisted I stay with her for a few days on my way back.

I happily agreed to everything.

CHAPTER TWENTY-SEVEN

FERRY

---◄○►---

THE NEXT FEW days passed much as the first two had. The sky remained dark and foreboding. We walked to the wharf only to see the waves breaking over it and sending salt spray high into the air. At home we prepared meals and Elizabeth taught me to bake molasses buns, sticky toffee pudding, and raisin pie. Our card games continued, but we stopped keeping score; we played just for the fun of it.

After five days Elizabeth returned to work and it was my turn to keep the wood stove burning, wash the dishes, and shop for groceries. As much as I wanted to get on my way, I was having a great time with my new friend. Actually, she was more than a friend. She was more like a mother—the kind I had always wanted. She listened to me, treated me like an adult who could think for herself, and accepted me for who I was. Sometimes I pretended she was my real mother and I was taking care of our real house.

Then on day seven, the wind dropped and the forecast called for calmer seas. Once more we walked to the wharf to talk to the ticket agent.

"There's a window in the weather, so the ferry is sailing at eleven this morning."

We ran home to grab my school bag and to pack a lunch and supper for the trip. The next thing I knew, we were at the gangway.

"Write to me and let me know how things are going at your grandparents' house. I'll also want to know if you find Amelia Earhart. Edwina, Ann, and Maude will want to know, too." The ferry whistle groaned and we both jumped. Elizabeth grabbed me in a tight hug. "God bless you and bring you safely back to me."

I walked up the gangway. Elizabeth was still waving when I reached the deck. With tears running down my cheeks, I waved back. Oh, how I wished I could run back to the security of her arms. But this was my one chance to find Amelia. It was now or never.

Elizabeth got smaller and smaller as we sailed out of the harbour. I waved until she was no longer visible. I clutched the railing until the cold wind and roll of the ferry sent me inside.

The large room on the upper deck had windows on two sides. Benches lined the walls, and there was a kitchen at one end with a large window for ordering food. A few tables and chairs sat in front of it. I guessed that was so we could eat more easily. A woman with a little boy on her lap, an older man and his wife, three girls in their twenties, and a well-dressed lady were the only other passengers in the room. Since I'd never been on a ferry, I supposed there could be others in different parts of the boat.

A man in a white jacket appeared in the kitchen window. "Sommit to eat, miss?" he asked.

I hesitated, wondering how much the food would cost.

"You'll be wantin' sommit on your stomach before we hit dem waves," he added.

"I have sandwiches, cookies, and an apple. Is that enough for the crossing?"

"Aye, but it's some heavy on yer stomach. Soup, crackers, and tea would do ye more good."

I asked how much, and he said one shilling. I knew I could afford that, so I sat down. The onion soup was thick and hot. I ate my crackers with jam and drank my tea. A few of the other passengers joined me, and we chatted while we ate. They had soup and tea, too.

"Them waves gets some high out where the wind sweeps across hundreds of miles," the old man next to me said.

"I'm off to my cabin as soon as I finish this," the well-dressed lady told me. "The lower you are on this ferry, the less the roll."

"I suppose ye'll not be back up here till de morn," the cook said. The lady laughed and replied, "Not on your life, b'y. It's the bunk for me."

In another hour the chairs and tables were sliding from one side of the room to the other. A sailor came in, tied them together, and pushed them into one corner. The passengers were all on the benches because they were nailed to the walls. The woman with the baby was having an awful time. He was throwing up and she was holding him at arm's length to keep her clothes clean. One of the girls clamped a hand over her mouth and ran out of the room. I presumed she was heading to the bathroom.

Two hours later the waves were as high as the side windows. A sailor mopped vomit off the floor as fast as he could. The smell was horrible, and my stomach churned. I'd have loved to go out on the deck for some fresh air, but I was afraid I'd get washed overboard.

Suddenly my stomach felt like it was coming up into my throat. I ran for the bathroom, but the sound of retching and a worse smell greeted me. Every sink was plugged with vomit, and when I turned to the toilet I saw it was plugged, too. I gagged, clamped my hand over my mouth, and just reached the outside door before I threw up on the deck. Another roll of the ferry and the door slammed shut in my face. It was just as well because a wave thumped against the closed door.

The big room and the bathroom were more than I could bear, so I lay in the empty hallway between them. With tightly clasped hands, I prayed that no one would throw up on me on their way to either location.

"Come, maid." Someone was gently shaking my arm. I looked up and saw the cook.

"I've got a place for ye in de kitchen," he said.

He helped me to my feet and guided me back into the big room. Other passengers were lying on the benches, with their arms over their faces. The little boy was snuggled in a blanket on the floor. The smell of vomit still lingered.

"Aren't you sick, too?" I asked the cook.

He laughed. "Not after thirty years at sea. I were ten when me dad took me down to de Labrador. Dis be calm seas to me."

We continued on to the kitchen where it was clean and warm. He poured me a cup of hot water from the kettle and told me to sip it slowly when it cooled. Then he told me about his four daughters. The youngest one, Mary, was about the same age as me. If his Mary were travelling on her own, he'd want someone to take care of her the way he was taking care of me.

After the hot water stayed in my stomach, he gave me a few dry crackers to eat. I was feeling so much better my eyes started to close. Albert, that was the cook's name, told me to put my head on the table and get a few hours sleep. He would play solitaire and see to the other passengers for the rest of the night.

———◀◦▶———

From somewhere far away I became aware of voices. My eyes opened and closed a few times before I could focus on Albert again. He stood in the kitchen window, pouring tea into half a dozen mugs. I stretched and stood up. It took me a few seconds to realize I wasn't falling from side to side.

Albert turned around and smiled at me. "Just a few more hours to North Sydney, Ginny."

I drank a cup of tea and ate a few more dry crackers while he told me what to watch out for when I left the boat.

"Mind now ye keep yer money in yer boot. Yer not in Harbour Grace anymore. No one out der knows ye and ye got no family to protect ye here."

CHAPTER TWENTY-EIGHT

BOSTON

———◄◦►———

THE TRAIN TRIP from North Sydney to Boston was quick and easy. Once I was in the Boston station, I went to the information desk and showed the lady the address I had for Amelia. She said the address was in the area of Denison House. Her words made me smile. From reading Pat's newspaper articles, I knew Amelia worked there. The lady drew me a map, and I thanked her before I left.

My heart was racing as I walked through the front doors and turned right, as she had indicated. I would soon be talking to Amelia Earhart! At the first intersection I turned right and at the next one I turned left. As I got away from the station, the streets seemed to be getting narrower and there were fewer people around. Large buildings with soot-covered windows closed in on me. Although I felt uneasy I told myself the information lady wouldn't have sent me in this direction if it were dangerous.

With the map held out in front of me, I walked on. It was not long before I noticed something strange. My winter boots were not making any sound on the pavement, and yet I heard footsteps. I slowed down and the footsteps slowed down. When I sped up, they sped up, too. I stopped and turned around.

Someone grabbed me by the shoulder strap on my school bag and swung me violently around. I lost my balance and landed on both knees. I could see him now—he had black hair and clothes, and a sailor's bandanna covered the lower part of his face.

He stuck his hand in each of my coat pockets. Then he grabbed my school bag and emptied it. "Where's the money?"

"I don't have any."

"Ya just got off the train, so ya got to have money."

"I'm only a kid."

"Yer gonna be a dead kid if ya don't hurry up."

He pulled out a knife and pressed it against my side. The point went right through my heavy wool coat. I winced and pulled off my boot. He thrust in his hand and pulled out my money—all of it. He threw my boot back to me and told me to get lost. I pulled it on and ran as fast as I could.

After a few blocks I slowed down and glanced over my shoulder. He was nowhere to be seen. I threw my head back and sucked as much air as I could into my lungs. Slowly, my heartbeat returned to normal, and I looked at my surroundings. With shaking hands I unfolded the crumpled map. I couldn't believe I held onto it throughout the robbery.

I walked to the closest intersection. Without realizing it I must have run in the direction of the train station. This was where I made one of my right turns.

Back at the information desk, I realized how badly my legs were shaking. I burst into tears when I tried to tell the lady what had happened to me. She rushed over and put her arm around my shoulders.

"My poor girl," she said. "You could have been killed." She gave me a hanky to dry my eyes and blow my nose.

She offered to call the police but said they probably wouldn't do anything. Robberies took place every day in these hard times. She sat me in her chair and leaned on the desk. She asked to see the map. I handed her the crumpled paper.

Quickly she clamped her hand over her mouth. "Oh my dear Lord. What have I done? I should have had you turning left on Cross Street, not right. No wonder you ran into trouble. I sent you down near the docks!"

She asked me to forgive her and of course I did. Then she offered me fifty cents of her own money.

"I wish it were more, but this is all I can afford at the moment," she said.

"I'll be all right. I'll go to my grandparents' house now," I replied.

"If you give me their address, I promise I'll be more careful with my directions."

With a new map in my hand, I left the station once more. This route looked more promising than the last one. The streets were wider and the properties were dotted with trees and flowers. After a long walk, I stood in front of Mom and Pop Davis's house. Mom Davis opened the door when I rang the bell.

Rather than saying *Ginny, what a pleasant surprise,* she grabbed my arm and pulled me into the house. "You wretched girl. Your mother is worried sick about you. Her telegram said you stole her money and ran away!"

She slammed the door closed behind me. Without another word she dragged me into the kitchen where Pop Davis was sitting at the table.

"So you did show up here," he said.

"And here she'll stay until her mother arrives to get her," Mom Davis said. Not a cup of tea or a slice of bread and butter before I was locked in a bedroom off the second-storey hall. I sat on the bed and wondered how I could've been so dumb. When Mom got Elizabeth's letter, she must have thought there was a chance I'd head this way. She was the one who sent word to look out for me.

Well, if Mom Davis thought I was staying there, she was foolish. I jumped up from the bed to find a way out, but, before I took a single step, I slowly sank back down. I just didn't have the strength to carry on. My head hurt and so did my knees. I lay down on my side and curled into a tight ball.

After two days of imprisonment, I was feeling more like my old self. The only time I had been let out was to use the toilet and take a bath. But Mom Davis had washed my clothes, mended my stockings, and fed me. I was amazed at how much she and Mom were alike—their tone of voice, the expressions they used, and their abrupt way of dealing with children. I couldn't say that I would have enjoyed growing up there. Now that I thought about it, I imagined Mom didn't have much fun here, either.

Thinking about Mom reminded me that I had to get out of there before she arrived. I had time to work out a plan, and there was no reason to delay another day. When Mom Davis dropped off my breakfast, I ate everything on the tray. I'd need all my strength and determination if I was going to escape.

The bedroom window looked down on the back laneway. With the chenille bedspread I made a knot around the leg of the large oak bed. I opened the window and sat on the sill with my legs hanging outside. This was the part I hadn't completely worked out. With both hands I grabbed onto the bedspread and gently swung myself over the sill. Now I was facing the outside wall. Thank goodness the nubs of cotton on the bedspread were large. They stopped my hands from slipping. I wasn't sure what to do with my legs, so I wrapped them around the bedspread the best I could.

By opening my fingers slowly, I began to slide downward. When I started moving too quickly, I tightened my grasp on the cotton nubs and slowed down. Four feet from the ground, I passed the kitchen window. Who should look up from the sink but Mom Davis. Her eyes and mouth opened wide at the same time. She was probably yelling for Pop Davis.

There was no time to lose; I dropped into the laneway and landed on my feet. My legs were moving within a second, and I ran at top speed when I heard, "Come back here, you wretched girl!"

Five minutes later I had left the house well behind me. Slowing down helped me get my breath back and allowed me to start reading the street signs. This time I turned left on Cross Street and continued on to Denison House. I rang the doorbell and a young girl led me to the director's office. A grey-haired lady got up from behind her desk and shook my hand when we introduced ourselves.

"Amelia hasn't been here for months," she said.

"But I sent her a letter to this address a few weeks ago."

"I forward all her mail to her husband's address in Rye, New York," the woman explained. "You'll have to go there if you want to see her."

She gave me a new set of directions. I had no choice but to leave. Outside the door I paused and looked around. Without money, I didn't know how I was going to carry on.

I walked to a nearby park and sat on a bench. I had to think of a new plan before it got dark. Since the robbery I didn't seem to be as brave as I used to be. After examining and rejecting a number of options, I realized the train station was the only place I could go.

The same lady was at the information desk, so I explained my predicament to her. She pulled a chair over to her desk and told me to sit there until she got back. When she returned she had a man in a uniform with her. She told me he was a friend who owed her a favour. He was going to sneak me onto the train from Boston to New York City. Once I got there I would need to ask for directions to Rye. The information lady shook my hand and wished me luck. I thanked her, but she told me it was the least she could do because, after all, it was her fault I lost my money.

The man in the uniform turned out to be a conductor. This was the beginning of his shift, so I was meeting him at the right time. We walked out on the platform together and he asked me to sit on a bench until he signalled me to enter the train. According to the railroad clock, half an hour passed before the platform started filling with people.

The conductor helped them lift their bags onto the train until the platform was empty again. Then he signalled me from the doorway and I walked onto the train. When he collected the tickets, he punched a blank piece of cardboard and with a wink handed it to me.

I was on my way to New York City.

CHAPTER TWENTY-NINE

RYE, NEW YORK

—◁◦▷—

I THOUGHT THE train station in Boston was big until I walked into the one in New York City. The ceiling soared a hundred feet over my head and stairways led up and down. People rushed in all directions without so much as a *pardon me* when they bumped into me or stepped on my foot.

I went directly to the information desk and asked for directions to Rye. The lady said my best bet was to take the bus because the town was thirty miles away. I told her my dad was going to drive. She took out a map and marked the route in red pencil. In fact, I had no choice but to start walking. I asked the lady for the route from the station to the big highway and she supplied that as well. I thanked her and began the next step in my quest to find Amelia.

New York City was huge! I was nervous after my experience in Boston. I didn't like to think about what would have happened if the robber hadn't found any money. He might have stabbed right through my coat, and me, too. But there

155

was one difference between the two cities. In New York people filled the streets. I would just stay where there was a lot of activity.

It was late afternoon when I got to the big highway. Cars whooshed by in both directions at a speed I had never seen before. Occasionally someone honked and I jumped toward the ditch. In most cases the drivers didn't seem to notice me.

After a few hours of walking, it was getting dark and too dangerous to stay along the side of the road. To make matters worse, it was starting to rain. I remembered passing a culvert under the road about half a mile back, so I turned around.

Fortunately, the rain stayed light until I got to it. I bent over and walked in. It was much darker in there, so I felt my way along for a few feet. The ground was dry and the side of the tunnel felt like cement. I sat down and leaned my head against it. From somewhere I heard the soft sound of water running. The bridge must have been over a small stream. If it stayed at its current level, I would be fine, but the rain had begun falling hard. Occasionally I heard the swish of a car overhead as it ran through a puddle.

I didn't think I would be able to sleep because of another sound I heard. Persistent rustling in the dry grass made my heart pound. "Please don't let it be rats," I whispered. It was so dark I couldn't see any eyes, but I was sure they were looking at me.

During the night the rustling sounds woke me. On one occasion I found myself lying in the grass with something tickling my cheek. I jumped up thinking it might be a whisker! But soon my eyes began to close and I had to sit down again.

◦

The next thing I knew, the tunnel was filled with light. My need for sleep had obviously been greater than my fear of rats. I crawled out and blinked in the morning sun. I was hungry and tired and a lump was forming in my throat. To hold back the tears, I thought of Amelia's 1928 transatlantic flight. It was true she was only a passenger, but it did take twenty hours and forty minutes to reach Burry Port, Wales. If I wanted to be a pilot, I'd have to toughen up.

I swallowed the lump, dusted off the back of my coat, and climbed up the hill to the side of the road. I would just keep putting one foot in front of the other until I got to Rye.

I had been counting my steps and the rhythm was hypnotic. But the blast of a car horn jolted me out of my trance. The car pulled over onto the shoulder about twenty feet in front of me. An old lady stepped out and waved to me. I walked toward her, and the closer I got, the more she smiled. She was wearing a navy blue suit, white gloves, and a pink flowered hat over her short white hair.

"Where are you going, my dear?" she asked.

I stopped a few feet from her. "Rye, New York," I replied.

"My husband and I would be happy to have you join us, but you'll have to sit in the back with Buddy."

I walked closer to the car and peeked in. I burst out laughing when I saw Buddy. He was the biggest orange cat I had ever encountered. Although I was a little nervous about joining strangers, I decided to trust Buddy's owners. If they seemed harmful in any way, I would threaten to throw Buddy out the window. Anyone who fed a cat that much must love him!

Mr. and Mrs. Phillips were from New York City. They were travelling through Rye to get to their daughter's house in Albany. Mrs. Phillips explained that Albany was farther north. After we chatted for a while, Buddy curled up on my lap. I scratched him behind the ears, and he closed his eyes and purred. When a cat this big purred, he sounded like a small engine. Every now and then Mrs. Phillips turned around and smiled at us. It was a pleasant way to travel, until we stopped for lunch.

What a struggle I had to shift Buddy's weight off my lap. Every time I moved he dug his claws into my legs. Mrs. Phillips had to crawl into the back seat and loosen his paws one at a time. Then we had to quickly close the car door before he could follow us into the restaurant.

Mr. Phillips insisted on paying for my meal and, I confess, nothing had ever tasted so good. To apologize for interrupting Buddy's nap, I took him a few scraps of roast beef from my plate. He curled up on my lap again, and we were on our way.

By two in the afternoon, we reached Rye and went through the same process to free me from Buddy's grip. When we were outside the car, I told Mrs. Phillips I was looking for Amelia Earhart. She told me I needed to go to the Putnam house. "It's called Rocknoll, but you'll be lucky to find her there. She flies all over the country, you know."

She pointed to a dirt road and wished me luck. I thanked her and Mr. Phillips for their kindness and waved goodbye. With food in my stomach and Amelia close by, I picked up the pace.

CHAPTER THIRTY

THE PUTNAM HOUSE

─◄o►─

I KEPT CHECKING the weather as I walked. Grey, low-hanging clouds scurried across the sky, but the road was dry and free of cars. The scenery changed from a few scattered houses to open fields and stands of bare trees. Evergreens added some colour to an otherwise brown and gray landscape.

When I started to tire, I employed the method I'd used earlier to keep moving: I put one foot in front of the other and counted my steps. But I had the same problem as yesterday. Every time I got past two hundred, I thought of Amelia, or flying lessons, or my sore feet. When that happened I lost count and had to start all over again.

At two hundred for the fifth or sixth time, the first huge drop of rain hit my face. In a matter of minutes, the clouds released a deluge. I ran for cover in a clump of pine trees. The branches held the water for a while and then began to leak.

I decided to keep walking since I was getting wet standing still. Within ten minutes I was soaked through. The dirt road was turning to mud and my boots stuck with every step. Worst of all was the cold rain running off the brim of my hat and down my back.

After a few more two hundreds, my teeth started to chatter. The house couldn't be much farther or Mrs. Phillips would have told me it was a long walk. It had to be around here somewhere.

I rehearsed what to say when I got there. "I'd like to speak to Amelia Earhart, please."

That sentence replaced the counting, and it seemed to spur me on. "I'd like to speak to Amelia Earhart, please. I'd like to speak to Amelia Earhart, please." I closed my eyes and kept walking.

By then I was barely lifting my feet. I longed to lie down and sleep for a few hours, but I knew I had to keep moving. I thought of the train trip from Harbour Grace; Elizabeth, Edwina, Ann, and Maude waiting in Port aux Basques for news; Albert, the cook on the ferry to North Sydney; the robbery in Boston; and the ride with Mr. and Mrs. Phillips—and Buddy—and I knew I couldn't stop now. My mind went into a kind of trance, and the only thing I heard was the squishing of my boots in the muck.

Sometime later the sound of a dog barking made me open my eyes. The dog stood in front of a stone house that fit Mrs. Phillips's description. I turned into the driveway and the black dog greeted me. The more I patted its head, the faster its tail wagged. The dog led me up the long driveway. We passed gardens that were free of snow. Green shoots poked up through the ground and small yellow and purple flowers bloomed in clumps. *April showers, bring spring flowers*, I thought.

We walked around a large black car and followed a stone walkway to the front door. I rang the doorbell and a round, grey-haired woman in an apron answered.

"I'd like to speak to Amelia Earhart, please."

"Who is it, Mrs. Waddell?" a woman's voice called from inside the house.

"Someone who looks like a drowned cat," Mrs. Waddell replied.

The next thing I knew, Amelia Earhart was standing in the doorway. My legs gave out. I dropped to my knees and sat back on my heels. The black dog sat beside me and licked my cheek. I'd done it. I had found Amelia Earhart.

Amelia and Mrs. Waddell rushed down the steps and lifted me to my feet.

"Right you are, child," Mrs. Waddell said. "Up these steps you come."

"George!" Amelia shouted into the house.

Two men joined us as we walked through the door.

"Who's this?" the one with glasses asked.

"I'm Ginny Ross from Harbour Grace, Newfoundland."

Amelia looked at him and he looked at the other man.

"Never mind who she is," Mrs. Waddell said. "A hot bath and dry clothes are what she needs now."

"Of course," Amelia said. "We can talk later."

Mrs. Waddell led me up the stairs to a bathroom on the second floor. She filled the tub and helped me peel off my wet clothes. I eased into the hot water until only my face showed above the bubbles. When I sat up, Mrs. Waddell scrubbed my hair with a wonderful-smelling shampoo. She poured water over my head until my hair was squeaky clean.

With a towel wrapped around me, she sent me to a bedroom down the hall where I found a white shirt, a pair of pants, a pair of boy's underwear, a belt, and socks lying on the bed. I put them on and combed my hair with my fingers. It was a bit longer than it had been when I left home. It felt wonderful to be clean and warm again. As I looked in the mirror over the dresser, I couldn't help but notice that I was dressed just like Amelia.

With Mrs. Waddell leading the way, we walked downstairs to the kitchen. I asked her whose clothes I was wearing and she said they belonged to Mr. Putnam's son, David. She told me she would have my clothes washed and dried by the following morning. That was when she noticed I wasn't wearing David's slippers and sent me back upstairs to get them.

When I returned to the main floor, I heard voices to my left.

"It's an omen, George." I recognized Amelia's voice.

One of the men laughed. "You and your omens. You're just superstitious."

"How many people from Harbour Grace, Newfoundland, have shown up at our door since we started planning this project?" Amelia asked.

"She's got a point, George," the other man replied.

I saw Mrs. Waddell at the end of the hall, so I turned and headed toward the kitchen. As quickly as I could, I ate the toast and drank the hot chocolate she had prepared. I was anxious to return to the parlour.

When I'd finished, I thanked her and she took me back to Amelia. We stood in the archway that led into the parlour. Amelia and the two men were bending over a round table in front of one of the many windows. They looked up in unison, and the men folded up the large piece of paper they were studying.

"How are you feeling, Ginny?" Amelia asked.

"Much better, thank you."

Mrs. Waddell left and Amelia invited me to sit on the sofa. She held her hand out to the man wearing glasses. "This is my husband, George Putnam. And this is our friend, Bernt Balchen." She held out her hand to the other man, who was putting the paper into his briefcase. I could see now it was a map.

"How do you do?" I said. They both shook my hand.

Amelia sat down beside me and the men sat in chairs opposite us.

"You've come a long way, Ginny," George said. "How did you get here?"

I started with Mom insisting I quit school and go out to work full-time. I continued with all my stops along the way—Port aux Basques, Boston, New York City, and finally, Rye. I mentioned all the people I'd met, including the thief in Boston. I ended my story by saying, "I want to be a pilot just like your wife, but I don't know how or where to get flying lessons."

"Why do you want to be a pilot?" Amelia asked.

I told her about Uncle Harry and myself fixing Aunt Rose's car, about my ground school lessons with him, and finally about how I felt when I sat in Mr. Mears's plane. Of course, I left out the part about him blaming me for the crash.

"I remember your letters now, Ginny," Amelia said with a smile.

"How does your Uncle Harry know so much about planes?" Bernt asked.

"He's the airstrip supervisor and he just loves planes," I explained. "And so do I, Miss Earhart. I know I can be a good pilot. I just need a chance."

Amelia looked at her husband. "George, is there some way we can help Ginny set up her flying lessons?"

"Not right now," he replied. "We already have a big project we need to complete. Maybe in the future you can contact her, when we move on to our next project."

"Yes, of course," Amelia said. "That might just work for her."

Bernt cleared his throat and said they'd better get going.

Amelia had a number of speaking engagements over the next few days. She turned to me and reached in her purse. She handed me a ten-dollar bill and told me to use it to get back home. I started to object, but she tucked the money into my hand.

"I'll be in touch with you as soon as our current project is over," she said. "I'm sorry to hear things are so difficult at home. If you have to quit school to help your family, that's fine. It just delays your plans. It doesn't end them. More important than anything is that you keep training with your uncle until the time is right to finish school and start pilot training."

She slipped something else into my hand and said it was for good luck. I looked down at a small, silver four-leaf clover. I thanked her and closed my hand tightly. Bernt stood up. We did the same and started to move toward the front door. I felt tears building up in my eyes again. Amelia Earhart was holding my hand, and some time in the future she was going to help me set up flying lessons. I couldn't say a word.

Amelia called down the hall: "Mrs. Waddell." When she joined us at the door, Amelia asked her to give me a good supper and an early bedtime. Bernt offered to drive me to New York City the next day to catch the train to Boston and then on home.

I brushed the tears off my face. "Thank you. I won't let you down."

Amelia gave me a hug. "I know you won't, Ginny Ross from Harbour Grace, Newfoundland."

After a few minutes of putting on coats and carrying suitcases out to the car, Mrs. Waddell and I waved as they drove away. I pinched myself to make sure I wasn't dreaming.

CHAPTER THIRTY-ONE

HOME

THE TRIP HOME was blissfully uneventful—no robbery, no confinement at Mom and Pop Davis's, and no rough seas on the ferry. I missed seeing Albert, the cook, because he had two days off. But Elizabeth was at home when I arrived. We spent a few glorious days together—cooking, playing cards, and visiting with Edwina, Ann, and Maude. Then I was on my way again.

I kept thinking about my time at Amelia's. What kind of omen was it when someone from Harbour Grace showed up at her door? What was her next big project? What was her project after that? Would she remember me? How could she help me? I thought I knew the answers to some of these questions, but I was afraid to say them out loud in case I was wrong. I would just have to wait and see what developed.

When the train pulled into the station at Harbour Grace, I stepped into a familiar world covered in a thin layer of snow. I decided to walk along Harvey Street and down Victoria to have a look at the store before I joined the others at the hotel. Imagine my surprise when I approached the store and saw a light shining through the front windows.

When I opened the door, I found an oil lamp glowing on the long counter. Llew looked up from the inventory book and rushed over to hug me. "Where have you been?"

"I went to see Amelia Earhart in Boston, but then I had to go on to New York."

"Were you successful?"

"Yes!"

He went to hug me again but changed his mind. Instead, he shook my hand vigorously.

"I'll give you all the details later," I said. "Right now I want to know why you're here."

"Things are pretty desperate. Your Nana is fading away. She still won't eat or sleep. Doc Cron says she had a complete nervous breakdown after your papa died."

I was startled. "Why isn't she at the hotel with the rest of the family?"

"She refused to leave the store when your Aunt Rose and Uncle Harry came for them. She thinks your papa is still here. The rest of the family stayed with her. They're upstairs. Your dad is the only one at the hotel."

I walked over to the pot-bellied stove and slumped down on one of the chairs. Llew pulled up another chair and sat beside me.

"I was so sure they'd all go to the hotel."

Llew shook his head. "It would have been better."

"What about Mom?" My mind often flashed back to the dream where I saw her crying in the store after Dad walked out the front door.

"She's at her wit's end. Sometimes when I come in after school, she's crying. She tries to cover it up, but I can see the desperation in her eyes. She let me go because she has no money to pay me. But I come in to make sure they have a little heat in the store and wood for the stove in the kitchen."

I took his hand. "Thank you."

"They're like family." He shrugged. "It's the least I can do for your papa. He always treated me like one of his own."

I released Llew's hand and stood. "I better go up now."

Llew told me he would leave and that I could lock up behind him. He said I would need the oil lamp to see my way upstairs. Mom couldn't pay the electric bill.

As he walked through the door, he paused.

"Billy has been stealing. Marbles, pencils, and erasers aren't what people are buying these days, and yet they're disappearing."

Llew said he would find scolding Billy difficult, even if he caught him red-handed. When there was no one in the store, he'd found him crying behind the short counter. He sat beside him and asked what was wrong, but Billy just shook his head. Llew said that between Nana, Dad's silence, and Mom's yelling, Billy was all but forgotten.

Before I closed the door, I slipped money into Llew's hand to replace some of what he loaned me. "Amelia gave me money to get home and I still have some left."

He shook his head and pressed it back into my hand. "You'll need it."

We said good night and he disappeared into the darkness. I took a deep breath to prepare myself for what I was going to face upstairs.

The kitchen was just as I had left it. Nana sat in her rocker, Billy talked to his toy soldiers at one end of the table, and Mom sewed at the other end. Another coal oil lamp glowed between them.

Nana looked up and whispered, "Ginny?"

Billy ran to me and threw his arms around my waist. I put my lamp on the table and hugged him back. When he looked up at me, I ruffled his hair. Nana extended her arms and I knelt down for her hug.

"Where have you been?" Mom yelled. She took a piece of paper from the drawer in the table and waved it in my direction. "Mom Davis's telegram said that you ran away from there, too!"

I stood up and faced her. "I went to see Amelia Earhart."

"Those damn planes again. I told you—"

"But I'm back." I looked her in the eye with what I hoped was a determined expression.

Mom paused and then sighed. "Yes, you are. And I suppose you'll be wanting a bit of supper."

CHAPTER THIRTY-TWO

CHANGE

———◄○►———

THE NEXT MORNING I found a different atmosphere in the kitchen. Mom was making tea and toast. When I joined Billy at the table, Nana stood beside her rocker before she walked haltingly to the cutlery drawer. She set the table, and within minutes we tucked into toast with blueberry jam and some tea. Even Nana!

I was still surprised by Mom's reaction to my return. At the very least I expected yelling, blaming, and, possibly, a good slap across the face. Maybe this meant she was going to start treating me more like an adult and respecting what I wanted to do with my life.

Mom got up and added more boiling water to the teapot. When she returned to the table she looked directly at me. "You better go to school until the end of the week. That way everyone will know where you've been, and I won't have to repeat the story over and over when people ask. Just leave out the part about Amelia Earhart."

It seemed I was wrong. The idea of treating me like an adult was over already. Every time I thought I'd taken a small step forward in my relationship with her, she reminded me that I hadn't moved at all. *Maybe I should accept the fact she will never change*, I thought. The notion made me sigh with disappointment, but if she noticed it she didn't say a word. The silence went on for some minutes.

It was easier to stand up to her last night when she was yelling at me. In this light she looked different. Dark circles under her eyes and the way she slouched in her chair made her look older and more tired. Maybe this wasn't the right time to declare my independence. A safer topic might be better.

"I'll go to see Aunt Rose at noon to tell her I'm back and ready to work," I said.

"The money will be a big help." Mom sat up straighter in her chair. "Robert McFarlane still brings in fish and rabbits. When he can spare them, Mr. Stevenson brings eggs and winter vegetables. I have a few tinned goods in the store and a few preserves in the storage room. I've been doing my best to carry on since you left."

Her last sentence hit me like a slap across the face. In spite of the way she treated me, was it possible she was doing her best?

"Coal and electricity are the worst shortages," she added.

"Llewellyn put my bed next to the grate in the floor in Mom and Dad's room," Billy said, "and we get the heat coming up from the kitchen."

I smiled at him and then at Mom. They needed me.

"It's good to be home," I said.

Nana squeezed my hand. I thought of what Amelia had said: I was just delaying my plans, not giving them up. I hoped Uncle Harry would be willing to continue my aviation lessons, because I might be out of school for a long time.

When breakfast was over, Billy and I walked out the front door together. He reached for my hand and I looked down at him and smiled.

"I like it better when you're around, Ginny," he said.

"I'm staying right here, so don't you worry." I bent over and did up the strap on his hat before we started the climb up Victoria Street.

Jennie Mae waved to us from the school gate as we turned onto Harvey Street. Llew must have told her I'd come home last night. I told her the truth about the train trip. But I would save the story of seeing Papa for a time when Billy wasn't around. She glanced down at his hand in mine and gave me a puzzled look. I looked into her eyes for a few seconds longer than usual and then smiled. That was our signal for *I'll tell you later.*

When Billy continued to stand beside me, I knelt down and reassured him I wasn't going anywhere. "I'll meet you here to walk home for lunch."

"Promise?"

I crossed my heart and held up my right hand. "Promise."

He hugged me and ran toward his friends.

I told Jennie Mae how I found them when I came home and what Llew told me about Billy's life since I left. She nodded and agreed that life for most people had become worse in the time I'd been away. Her dad had less and less to share with those who needed it, and this worried him.

"But there is good news," I told her. "I found Amelia Earhart."

Jennie Mae's eyes opened wide and she clamped her hand over her mouth. I gave her all the details—good and bad. She squeezed my hand so tightly when I got to the part about Amelia that I winced in pain.

"Sorry," she whispered. "I'm just so excited I have to do something or I'll scream!"

"I wish I knew what project she is going to involve me in," I said.

"Do you think it will involve flying lessons?" Jennie Mae asked.

Before I could answer, a teacher rang the big brass bell and we all ran toward the school to line up. As the grade ones moved inside, Billy turned around and waved to me.

I knew I was home when I walked into the cloakroom. Damp wool and seal oil had never smelled so good. People crowded around and asked where I had been. I told them I went to see a friend in Port aux Basques, which was true. Elizabeth Harris was my new friend. They wanted to know all about the train, the food, and the sleeping arrangements.

I answered their questions until Miss Rorke shooed us into our seats and our morning routine began.

When the bell for recess rang, Miss Rorke asked me to stay behind. Pat Cron was the last to leave the classroom.

"You've got a lot of catching up to do," Pat said to me as she walked out the door.

Alice Brant was waiting for Pat in the hall. I noted that their friendship was still going strong and reminded myself to beware.

At noon I met Billy in the schoolyard and we walked to the store together. He said he would tell Mom I had gone to the hotel to show Aunt Rose and Uncle Harry I was back. I also wanted to tell them the truth about my trip, but I didn't mention this to Billy.

I burst into the hotel and dragged the two of them into the kitchen. They welcomed me with hugs and pats on the back. Then we sat down at the table and Aunt Rose poured tea for all of us.

"I was sure you or Mom would be on that snowplow and ready to take me home to Harbour Grace," I told Uncle Harry.

He laughed and said, "You obviously need more tutoring on direction before you become a pilot. That plow came from Port aux Basques, not Harbour Grace."

I covered my mouth with my hand. "It must have been the stress of being alone on a train that confused me."

"Right you are, Columbus," Uncle Harry replied.

We all laughed and then settled down to the sandwiches Aunt Rose put on the table. I showed them the six dollars I had left from the ten-dollar bill Amelia had given me.

"Getting a load of coal delivered and turning on the electricity seem to be the priorities," I said.

"Warmth and light will raise their spirits," Aunt Rose agreed.

"What about some supplies from Bowring Brothers?" I asked.

We had to discuss this for some time. Although supplies would give Mom something to trade for what we needed, the family seemed to be managing on Papa's goodwill. I told them what Mom said about Robert McFarlane and Mr. Stevenson. Uncle Harry thought I would be better to save whatever was left to continue heating and lighting the place. Then if it seemed we needed to buy supplies, we could do so. I asked him to keep the money for me and to arrange for the coal and electricity.

Aunt Rose offered me more hours working at the hotel but suggested I talk to Mom before I accepted. I told her I was allowed to return to school until the end of the week, and after that I would be available to work full-time. She agreed and said she would continue to give me my supper when I worked there. Neither of us mentioned Dad because we both knew she was feeding him, as well.

"Why is the hotel managing when so many businesses around town are closing?" I asked.

"No one is taking rooms or eating here, but the beverage room is doing well," she explained. "It's a sad fact that in hard times there always seems to be money for the whisky and beer."

We ate in silence for a few minutes, and then I turned to Uncle Harry. "Amelia wants me to continue my training with you."

"I have to admit, I've missed our sessions," he said.

I picked up Billy at the store, and all the way back to school I kept thinking, *My plans are delayed, not ended. My plans are delayed, not ended.*

CHAPTER THIRTY-THREE

LOUIS REICHERS

———◆———

W HEN BILLY AND I walked into the schoolyard after
lunch, everyone was talking about Louis Reichers.
His flight was announced by the Airport Trust at noon. He
would arrive from New York on May 13, between 5:00 A.M.
and 6:00 A.M. Depending on the weather, he would leave a
few hours later.

Jennie Mae, Llew, and I wandered around the schoolyard
together and talked about what I should do about his flight.
I told them Mom still seemed uncomfortable with any talk
about planes. However, she was relieved to have me back
and to have a source of money on a regular basis.

"You know as well as I do how your mom will react if she
finds out you're up at the airstrip," Llew said. "I think you
should skip the flight altogether."

"There are still three weeks before Reichers arrives," I said.
"Maybe if I assure Mom that watching a plane doesn't mean
I'm going to leave home again, she won't mind."

"That sounds reasonable to me," Jennie Mae said.

Llew just shook his head.

————◄◌►————

Right up until May 13, I watched for an opportunity to talk to Mom about Louis's flight, but we were getting along so well that I didn't want to set her off again. She was especially pleased with how warm and bright the house was again. I told her where the money came from, and she asked if there was more. I said we had a little but that it was for emergencies. She wasn't so pleased to hear Uncle Harry was keeping it in the safe at the hotel.

I made sure she saw that I wasn't going to Louis's early-morning landing. At the usual time, I left for the hotel. When I got there I ran up Cochrane Street, along Harvey Street, and up Victoria to the airstrip.

Uncle Harry told me that on the landing the tail skidded and threw up a loose rock. This slightly damaged the plywood covering the port stabilizer. Since Jennie Mae and I had resumed our aviation lessons, I knew exactly what he was talking about.

He assured me the damage could be repaired while the plane was being refuelled. Louis was at the hotel having a light breakfast, and Aunt Rose was probably making him sandwiches and coffee to take with him.

A few minutes later a car pulled up to the plane and,

sure enough, he got out with a Thermos and bundle of sandwiches. He waved to the crowd and entered the plane. We continued to wave as he rolled down the runway. The takeoff was picture perfect, with no crash landing into the boulders. He soared down the bay and disappeared into the bright sun.

I walked back to the hotel with Uncle Harry and we discussed the technical details of the takeoff. Instead of concentrating on my cooking and cleaning all morning, I was thinking about Louis's flight. I kept checking the time and guessing how far he'd already flown.

At noon I returned to our house to eat. Although Aunt Rose gave me my supper, I liked to go home during the day to see how everyone was managing. As I opened the front door, Alice Brant pushed past me with an eerie smile on her face. It was the same smile she had on her face before pushing me around at school.

Mom walked out from behind the counter and grabbed me by the shoulders. "You've got to let go of those planes and that insane idea that you're going to be a pilot." She shook me so hard I felt like my head would fly off.

I pulled away from her and shouted, "Why are you so against me being a pilot?"

"You haven't got what it takes!" she shouted back. "You're no Amelia Earhart!"

"I don't have to be beautiful and well dressed. I'm smart, I'm stubborn, and I'm not afraid to take risks."

"But when you fail, you'll be the laughingstock of the whole town."

"I don't care what people think or say about me." I looked at Mom with all the fire I felt in my heart. "I'm me, and if people don't like me the way I am, too bad for them!" I turned around and marched out the door.

Down the street, I saw Alice and three of her friends. Even at a distance I could identify Pat. I knew she liked to be the centre of attention and—I had to admit—I'd been getting a lot of that lately. She was obviously mad about it. I figured she was being encouraged by Alice and the other girls. But why was I blaming them? Pat didn't have to go along with them.

At the hotel, Aunt Rose listened to what had happened at home. She shook her head and gave me a hug. "You're right, you know. Maybe someday your mom will value the real you and not the well-dressed, polite lady she wants you to be."

"I'm not holding my breath."

Aunt Rose chuckled and put her arm around my shoulders while we walked into the kitchen.

"Is it possible Mom is trying her best and still treating me this way?"

"You've met her role model, Mom Davis."

"They *are* alike."

Aunt Rose sat down at the table and I joined her.

"Mother–daughter relationships are always complicated,

and you'll forgive me if I say I don't know anything about them," she said.

"You haven't been a mother, but you have been a daughter," I reminded her.

"My brothers, sisters, and I more or less raised ourselves. My mother was pregnant with my youngest sister when my father died. She had to take over the running of the Archibald Boot and Shoe Factory. At home we had a cook and a maid. I had a great deal of admiration for my mother, but I didn't see her much." Aunt Rose reached for my hand. "You're a smart young lady," she said. "You'll figure it out—even if your mom can't."

As I chopped vegetables for soup, I thought about what Aunt Rose said. I thought I was a pretty smart young lady, too, but I still had no idea how to deal with Mom. Thinking about her made me think of Louis's flight.

Llew's words came back to me: *Skip the flight.*

I should have listened to him. There would be more flights during the summer season, and Mom would be watching me like a hawk from now on.

#

CHAPTER THIRTY-FOUR

T HE NEXT DAY we found out Louis Reichers crashed into the sea off the coast of Ireland. Fortunately, a ship had been close by. He was rescued none the worse for wear, except for some facial cuts and a broken nose. Mom absorbed every detail about the crash in the newspaper.

"If the ship hadn't happened by, that man would have drowned," she said. Where I saw the happy ending, she saw the disaster.

Four days later Uncle Harry rushed into the hotel with news about the next flight for this season. Aunt Rose and I sat down at the kitchen table to hear all the details. Bernt Balchen would fly a plane from New Jersey on May 19. Ed Gorski, his mechanic, and a "third person" would rest in the back of the plane until they arrived in Saint John, New Brunswick. They would spend the night there, and then Bernt would fly to Harbour Grace on May 20. Although they gave the names of the two men, the official announcement didn't name the third person or the final destination.

I jumped to my feet and put my hands on my head. I knew who the third person was: Amelia Earhart! As I paced back and forth, I went over the clues. Bernt Balchen, a big project, an omen from Harbour Grace, and Amelia's words after her 1928 flight—"Next time I'll fly the plane myself." I collapsed onto a chair and looked at Aunt Rose and Uncle Harry.

"Amelia Earhart is going to make a solo transatlantic flight from Harbour Grace!"

They didn't even ask how I knew. They jumped up and hugged each other. Then they hugged me.

"That explains all the secrecy," Uncle Harry said.

"When do you think Amelia will be identified?" I asked him.

"I think they'll announce it right before they leave New Brunswick. As long as the weather stays good, she'll land here, refuel and rest for a few hours, and then take off to cross the Atlantic on the same day. That way no other woman will be able to beat her across the ocean and claim the title."

As it turned out, Uncle Harry was right. On May 20 there was still some question about the destination, but no one in Harbour Grace seemed to care. The fact that Amelia Earhart was arriving around two o'clock today was all that mattered. The news spread around town like wildfire.

I ran home at noon. I'd eat quickly and return to the

hotel as fast as I could. Aunt Rose said I could go to Amelia's landing and to her takeoff later in the day. Mom was in the store, so Billy and I ate our sandwiches in the kitchen with Nana.

"If my old legs were stronger, I'd be up that hill to see Amelia myself."

"You can see her at the hotel," I told her.

She smiled and nodded. "I might just do that."

As soon as we finished, I told Billy to wait for me while I got something from my room. I ran up the stairs and retrieved Amelia's silver four-leaf clover from the top shelf in my wardrobe. When I turned around, my door was closing. Then the key turned in the lock. I grabbed the handle and shook it as hard as I could.

"Let me out," I screamed. "Nana, help me!"

I kicked the door and pounded it with my fists, but there wasn't a sound from the hall. I continued calling for what seemed like an hour, but no one came. I slid down the door, buried my face in my hands, and cried.

Then it dawned on me. Mom was just repeating what Mom Davis did to me in Boston. Why didn't I see this coming? I knew how alike they were. Gently I thumped my head against the door. I couldn't believe I wouldn't be seeing Amelia again or asking what her next project was.

So why was I sitting here? I brushed the tears off my face and started pacing the room. *There must be a way out*, I thought. I opened the window and looked at the drop to the back garden. Even with the bedspread tied to the leg of my bed, it was too far to fall.

As I started pacing again, I became aware of a sound—a scratching sound from the other side of the door. I put my ear against it.

"Ginny?" a voice whispered. "Where does she keep the keys?"

"On a hook by the kitchen door," I whispered back.

I stood with my hands up to my mouth until I heard the key in the lock. The door opened, and Billy wrapped his arms around me.

"How will you get out of the house, Ginny?" he asked.

I knelt down and looked into his eyes. "You get Mom out of the store and I'll find a way," I assured him.

We walked to the landing on the second floor together. Then Billy smiled up at me and continued down to the store. I crouched at the top of the stairs and peeked under the banister. He ran past the long counter and shouted, "Bye, Mom!"

"Are you still here?" she asked.

He opened the front door and fell into the street. His screams had Mom running after him. I slipped down the stairs and across the store to the trap door. Nana turned around and I put my finger to my lips. She smiled and gave me the okay sign.

In seconds I stood on the ladder and pulled the door closed over my head. I was so glad I'd done this before.

Without banging an elbow or a knee, I was out the basement door and running up the side of the store to Water Street. I peeked out, but Mom and Billy must have gone back inside.

At Victoria Street, I turned the corner to get out of sight. Just above the railroad track, I could see and hear Aunt Rose on her megaphone.

"She's a spot in the sky now, but she'll be on the ground shortly," she called. "Lift those knees, my pets, or you'll miss her landing."

I did what she said, in the fastest time I'd ever run up that hill. I got to the airstrip just as Amelia approached the runway. With the rest of the children, I peeked through arms and legs to get a glimpse of the plane. When I still couldn't see, I got down on my hands and knees and crawled toward the runway. A few startled people jumped out of the way and then laughed and moved their legs. I finally got to the front of the crowd just as her plane touched down.

I watched the wheels contact the runway; there was a spray of gravel and we all cheered. As she got closer, I noticed something wrong but couldn't identify what it was. The wings were in line, the flaps were set, and the speed was good. I watched closely for a few more seconds.

Then I saw it. The right front wheel wasn't rotating properly. It jumped slightly on each turn. I'd have to tell Uncle Harry about this.

As soon as the plane came to a stop, the crowd surged forward with the men from the Airport Trust out in front. The side door opened and Amelia waved to the crowd. A cheer went up and we waved back. She wore a one-piece flying suit, and her short hair blew in the wind. Her face was so familiar to me now.

She stepped down and got lost in the throng of people. No one seemed to notice Bernt Balchen and Ed Gorski. Uncle Harry stood on the running board of Mike Hayes's taxi with Aunt Rose's megaphone up to his mouth.

"Stand back, folks! Miss Earhart's car is coming through."

I knew I should head to the hotel if I wanted to talk to her, but first I had to talk to Uncle Harry.

Once Amelia, Ed, and Bernt were on their way to file their flight plan, I looked for him. He stood next to the plane, with Mr. Stevenson, preventing the crowd from crossing the rope fence tied to the barrels. I told him what I saw and he checked the right front tire.

"I can't see anything," he said. "But I'll look at it again when Bernt and Ed return from the courthouse."

I nodded. "Good. I better get to the hotel."

I headed toward Victoria Street. Just as I got to Harvey Street, I looked down and saw Mom marching past the Crons' house. Her head was down and her arms were pumping vigorously.

CHAPTER THIRTY-FIVE

AMELIA AND ME

———◦———

ALL I NEEDED was for Mom to look up and see me. I ducked around the corner and ran down Harvey Street to Cochrane Street. I turned around and she was nowhere in sight. The Archibald Hotel was at the bottom of Cochrane Street, and five minutes later I was at the front steps.

Aunt Rose was walking along Water Street toward the hotel. I ran up to her and tried to catch my breath. "Mom—locked me in my room. Billy let…me out. Mom is probably on her way here."

"You let me deal with your mother," she said. "Wait in the kitchen until I get there."

I was puffing so hard, I flopped onto one of the chairs. I'd barely caught my breath when the door jerked open.

"I managed to cut her off and sent her up to the courthouse," Aunt Rose said. "She'll probably follow the crowd back down here, but we'll cross that bridge when we get to it."

She took my hand and patted it. "Don't you worry, my pet. I won't let her spoil things for you."

We heard voices in the entranceway and Aunt Rose opened the kitchen door. Over her shoulder she told me to stay put.

"All right, you lot," her voice boomed from the dining room. "Out you go. Miss Earhart needs something to eat and a little peace and quiet."

I leaned gently on the kitchen door and peeked out. Amelia was stepping out of her flying suit. I let the door close and stood next to the table with my hand on the back of a chair.

A few seconds later, Amelia walked in. Her face lit up with a smile when she saw me.

"Hello, Ginny Ross from Harbour Grace, Newfoundland," she said. "I bet you didn't expect to see me this soon."

"This is more than I dared hope for!"

She shook my hand and put her arm around my shoulders. "How was your trip home?"

"I'm happy to say it was very uneventful, thank you. This is my Aunt Rose. She owns the hotel."

Amelia shook her hand and Aunt Rose suggested we all sit down. While she passed tea and sandwiches, Amelia told us the meeting I saw in Rye was the one at which she, George, and Bernt agreed to her solo flight.

"I saw history in the making," I said.

"And you'll soon see more," Aunt Rose added.

Before anyone could reply we heard footsteps in the dining room.

"Bernt and Ed wanted to stay with the plane to supervise the refuelling, but Harry said he'd join me here," Amelia said.

The kitchen door banged open, and there stood—Mom. Her face was red, her hair was damp, and her chest was heaving as she gasped for air.

For a second the three of us stared at her. Then Aunt Rose got up and led Mom to the table. "I'm so glad you're here," she said. "Miss Earhart, may I present Ginny's mother, Renie Ross."

Amelia stood up and extended her hand. "A pleasure to meet you, Mrs. Ross."

Mom wiped her hand on her dress and offered it to Amelia. "Ah...the pleasure is mine."

"Won't you join us for tea and sandwiches?" Aunt Rose asked.

Mom brushed her damp hair off her face. "I suppose I have time for one cup."

She and Amelia sat down.

"Ginny is an extraordinary girl, Mrs. Ross," Amelia told Mom. "Very few girls think about flying, let alone make plans to take lessons."

It was the first time I'd seen Mom looking so confused. I knew what she would like to say, but she was talking to Amelia Earhart, the most famous aviatrix of all time.

"I remember when I was in Boston and a barnstormer took me up in his plane for a two-dollar ride," Aunt Rose said. She stood up with her arms outstretched and her eyes closed. "I can still feel the wind on my face and see the earth stretching out below me like a blue, green, and yellow patchwork quilt." She sat down and said that, if she weren't as old as she was, she would be doing the same thing as me.

Mom looked thoughtful as Amelia and Aunt Rose talked about the thrill of flying. Both agreed women were as capable as men and that soon female pilots would be completely accepted.

Mom agreed to a second cup of tea. "Forgive me, Miss Earhart, but you make flying sound like an everyday event."

Amelia nodded. "It's no more dangerous than going out to sea or driving a car."

"But Ginny is an unathletic thirteen-year-old girl," Mom pointed out. "What chance does she have?"

"She has the same chance as me," Amelia said simply.

I identified what we had in common. First, when she was seventeen, Amelia took an automobile mechanics course. She watched planes take off and land for a few years before she took her first flight. Then she was hooked and began to learn everything she could about planes.

"Ginny has accomplished at thirteen what I accomplished at twenty-one," Amelia said. "She'll have to finish school, of course, but then—as far as I can determine—she'll be ready for flying lessons."

Again we heard footsteps in the dining room. The kitchen door banged open.

"You were right!" Uncle Harry ran to the table, pulled me to my feet, and hugged me. "It was a piece of metal in the tire that was causing the bumping." He looked at Amelia. "Let me assure you, Miss Earhart, you did not pick it up on my runway. John Stevenson and I walked it at least five times before you landed."

"We thought it was just the rough gravel," Amelia said.

"You were lucky the tire didn't blow out," Uncle Harry told her. "It could have caused a crash." He went on to explain what I had seen.

"We couldn't see it ourselves at first, so we asked some of the men who were still standing around to help us. They rolled the plane forward a few inches at a time while Bernt, Ed, and I checked the tire. Lo and behold, there it was!"

Amelia moved Uncle Harry out of the way and hugged me herself. "How do you know so much about planes?"

I reminded her that Uncle Harry had been teaching me, and Amelia shook his hand.

"Thank you, Uncle Harry," she said.

We resumed our seats at the table. I noticed Mom's astonished expression.

"You mean Ginny really is capable of becoming a pilot?" she asked Amelia.

Amelia looked at me. "That's what Ginny has been trying to tell you."

There was silence while Mom took all of this in. Aunt Rose got up to re-boil the kettle, and Uncle Harry asked for tea and sandwiches to take to Bernt and Ed.

I looked back at Mom. She was staring at the table, slowly stirring her tea. Then she drank the last of it and announced she should get back to the store. She stood up and we did the same. Amelia extended her hand and Mom shook it.

"Safe landing, Miss Earhart," Mom said.

"Thank you, Mrs. Ross."

Before she opened the kitchen door, Mom looked back at us. The confusion was still evident in her eyes.

CHAPTER THIRTY-SIX

PREPARATIONS

———◦———

AMELIA KEPT SHAKING her head and telling me how amazed she was at the depth of my knowledge. Uncle Harry couldn't smile any wider if he tried. I knew he would love to stay around for all the compliments, but he had to get the food and tea up to Bernt and Ed at the airstrip. He said goodbye and told us he would see us soon.

"When you met George, Bernt, and me at Rye, you told us what your uncle was teaching you. But this practical demonstration convinces me more than ever that you are the perfect candidate for our next project."

"And what *is* your next project?" I asked eagerly. I held my breath and crossed my fingers on both hands.

"I want you to become a pilot and help me inspire other young women to do the same."

They were the words I had been hoping to hear ever since I got back from Rye. Then I heard Mom telling me that I'm no Amelia Earhart. My smile faded and I let go of Amelia's hand.

"I don't exactly look like you...."

"Ginny, I'm a painted doll because I have to be. I'm the flag bearer, which means I'm the one who has to attract attention to the idea that women can be successful pilots in a world that thinks aviation is for men."

"So Mom's not the only one."

Amelia laughed. "I'm afraid not." She reached across the table and squeezed my hands. "Have you ever seen me wearing my flying goggles?"

"No."

"That's because I look like a frog in them," she said. "Why do you think I smile with my mouth closed?" she asked. "Because you could drive a truck through the space between my front teeth."

Aunt Rose returned to the table with fresh tea. Amelia explained that most pictures of her were official photos in which her hair was done and she was wearing makeup. She told me that a pilot only needed courage, determination, and knowledge, and that I had all those qualities.

"Look how old you are and where you live. Still you haven't given up," she said.

"Does your family support you?" I asked.

"My mother does. My father isn't around much. I love him dearly, but I'm afraid he spends too much time indulging in his favourite drinks."

I looked at Aunt Rose and she nodded; she knew I was thinking about Dad.

Amelia looked at her watch and announced it was three o'clock. Time for her to take a nap. Aunt Rose stood up to show her to her room. I promised to wake her at 5:30 P.M.

I sat and thought about everything Amelia had said, until Aunt Rose bustled back into the kitchen.

"You'd better get that soup on the stove," she instructed. "Amelia told me she doesn't want anything but soup and tomato juice on her flight."

"I'm afraid we didn't convince Mom that I'm capable of learning to fly."

Aunt Rose looked over at me. "It's a lot for her to think about," she said. "Furthermore, from whence do you think you got your stubbornness, my lady?"

I smiled even though I was surprised by her comment. Was it possible Mom and I were more alike than I realized? I supposed it was stubbornness that kept me from giving up my dream of becoming a pilot. It was probably stubbornness that got me all the way to the Putnam house. And it would take stubbornness to keep me working until the time was right to finish school and take flying lessons. Maybe that was why Mom and I had so much trouble talking to each other.

I thought about this while Aunt Rose and I passed the rest of the afternoon making more sandwiches for the men to eat during the night. The next thing we knew, Mike Hayes arrived with his taxi. Bernt had received a telegram from the weather office predicting good flying on the route he had planned for Amelia.

Aunt Rose sent me upstairs to wake Amelia. When I tapped on the door, she asked who it was and then invited me in. She was sitting on the bed and asked me to take the chair across from her.

"I've been thinking about our next project to attract more women into aviation. It won't happen right away, but George and I have some good ideas. We would like to find a university to partner with. Girls could take academic subjects and flying lessons at the same time. That way they could graduate with a university degree and a pilot's license. Just think of what that could do for bright young women like you."

"It's what I've always dreamed of." I clasped my hands under my chin but quickly lowered them, in case I looked like an excited child instead of a bright young woman. "I can keep working for Aunt Rose and do my school work at night. I'll ask Miss Rorke to help me."

"If anyone can manage all that, Ginny, it's you," Amelia said. She stood up and gave me a quick hug. "Off you go, now, while I pull myself together."

Amelia came downstairs in her brown one-piece flying suit with her goggles and helmet in her hand. Aunt Rose handed her the Thermos of soup and told her I made it. Amelia smiled and reached for it. "This is the fuel I need to get to Paris!"

She shook hands with Aunt Rose and thanked her for her hospitality.

"Come on," Amelia said to me. "I'll give you a ride to the airstrip."

Aunt Rose handed me the tin of tomato juice and I followed Amelia into the back seat of Mike's taxi.

CHAPTER THIRTY-SEVEN

TAKEOFF

———◦———

WITHIN TWO MINUTES we were at the airstrip. The crowd cheered as the taxi stopped near the plane. Amelia stepped over me, opened the door, and got out. Then she turned to me and said, "You, too."

I emerged from the car to a decrease in the cheering. Instead, I heard, "Ginny Ross? It's Ginny Ross!"

"This way, Miss Earhart." Uncle Harry held out his arm to clear a path to where Bernt and Ed stood talking. Amelia took my hand and we ducked under the rope fence to join the two men. They used technical language to discuss the flight, and Amelia asked if I understood. When I told her I did, she smiled and patted me on the back.

After some minutes, Bernt and Ed walked to the plane for the final check and Amelia turned to me. "I think I saw your mom and brother in the crowd."

With her hand on my shoulder, we walked toward them. Amelia shook Mom's hand and then Billy's.

"Good luck," Mom said.

"Good luck from me, too," Billy added.

Amelia smiled and ruffled his hair. "Thank you."

She shook a few more of the hands extended toward her as we moved along the rope. I couldn't see Jennie Mae or Llewellyn, but I knew they were there somewhere. Then I saw Pat standing with her aviation scrapbook in her arms.

In spite of the way she'd been treating me lately, one truth remained: if it hadn't been for that book, I would never have learned so much about Amelia Earhart. I turned to Amelia and asked if she would mind meeting one more person. She glanced at the plane, where Bernt and Ed were still working, and agreed. She smiled at people as we walked and they wished her good luck or safe landing.

As we approached Pat, her face lit up with a toothy smile.

"This is my cousin, Pat Cron."

"It's an honour to meet you, Miss Earhart."

After they shook hands, Pat opened her book to a page with pictures and articles about Amelia and handed her a pen and asked if she would sign it.

"You know more about me than I do," Amelia said.

"Thank you, Miss Earhart," Pat replied. She beamed as she watched Amelia sign the page.

Amelia glanced back to the plane where Ed and Bernt were talking to Uncle Harry. "It's time for me to get down to business." She squeezed my hand. "I'll write when I get back from Paris."

The lump in my throat prevented me from saying anything but "thank you."

Amelia turned and walked to the plane while I ducked under the rope to join Pat.

"I can't believe Amelia Earhart is here," she gushed. "Thanks for introducing her to me."

I smiled at Pat. "You're welcome."

"We're lucky to see this," she continued. "Amelia's going down in the history books."

"Yes, she is."

"Are you really going to be a famous pilot, Ginny?"

"I'm going to be a pilot, but I don't know about famous. Maybe I'll leave the famous part to you."

She laughed and slipped her arm through mine. For the next half hour we watched in awe as Bernt, Ed, and Amelia walked around the plane with Uncle Harry doing the pre-flight check. At seven o'clock Amelia climbed through the hatch over the cockpit, and five minutes later the engine roared to life.

I closed my eyes and imagined I was behind her seat in the cockpit. I checked my gauges, oil pressure, tachometer, fuel, and compass. I lined up with the centre of the runway, checked my gauges one more time, noted the time, and then applied full throttle to begin my takeoff run.

With my heart pounding, I opened my eyes to watch Amelia. She bounced down the runway, keeping the tail down until she had enough speed to prevent it from swinging in the wind. With maximum thrust, the tail lifted and she was off the ground. At the end of the runway she soared into the grey light. We watched and waved until she disappeared.

People didn't move, even when the plane was a dot in the sky. Some talked about her safe landing in Paris. Others shook their heads.

Mrs. Crane, Llewellyn's mother, dabbed her eyes with a hanky. "She's so young and pretty—and capable, to be sure. But we may be the last people to see her alive."

CHAPTER THIRTY-EIGHT

THE LONG NIGHT

———◄O►———

I CAUGHT UP to Aunt Rose, who was walking with Mom and Billy. "May we come over to the hotel to wait for news?" I asked.

"That's up to your mom," Aunt Rose replied.

"No," Mom said. "I don't think that's a good idea."

"Please, please, please!" Billy jumped up and down in front of her. It was the most lively I'd seen him since I came home from New York.

Mom frowned. "We can't leave Nana alone."

"She can come too! Llew will help me get her down the stairs at the store," I offered. She turned her glare from Billy to me.

"And I'll call Mike Hayes to pick her up in his taxi," Aunt Rose added. She knew Mom wouldn't disagree with her.

By the time Llew and I helped Nana up the steps and into

the hotel, Bernt, Ed, and Uncle Harry were already sitting at one of the dining room tables talking to Mr. Gibson, the telegraph operator. He would be up all night sending and receiving messages. At that moment Bernt and Ed were composing a telegram for George Putnam, Amelia's husband, to tell him she took off safely.

Instead of sitting down with Llew and Nana, I crossed the entrance hall to the beverage room. It was crowded with men, but Dad sat alone at a table. He looked up and smiled when he saw me. "What are you doing in here?"

"I spoke to Amelia Earhart this afternoon," I told him. "She thinks I'm very capable of becoming a pilot, and she's going to help me."

"I wish your papa could have lived to see this day," he said. My eyes filled up with tears and Dad wiped his handkerchief quickly across his face to hide his own. The two of us sat in silence for a minute before Dad continued. "We've had a rough time since your papa died."

I looked at my hands and nodded. "We need your help, Dad."

This time he let the tears run down his face. "I feel so useless," he said. "I don't know how to run a store. Your papa made all the decisions, and I just followed his orders." He smiled and shook his head. "I wanted to join the merchant fleet and see the world, Ginny. But he and Nana wanted me to take over the store when they got too old to work. I stayed home, and I've regretted it ever since."

"I'm so sorry, Dad."

He shrugged. "That's ancient history now, Ginny." He wiped his face again with his handkerchief and handed it to me.

I dried my eyes and took a deep breath. "Then let's talk about the future."

He took my hand in his and smiled. I took his smile as agreement and continued.

"At least if you stay in the store, Mom will get a bit of a break," I said. "Maybe you can get Llew back, and, between the two of you, figure out what Papa used to do."

"It will be difficult with so little money coming in, but I suppose it's worth a try," he said.

I passed the balled-up hanky back to him. "Let's start with some food." I stood up, took his hand, and we walked into the dining room together.

Aunt Rose looked somewhat surprised to see Dad, but she waved him into the room. "May I get you a table, sir?" She took his elbow and showed him to the table where Uncle Harry, Ed, and Bernt were sitting. He gave her a quick peck on the cheek and sat down.

"This is my cousin Bill Ross," Uncle Harry said. The men shook hands and the conversation continued.

Before I sat down I asked Aunt Rose for one more favour. "May I go get Pat and Jennie Mae?"

She laughed and said, "The more the merrier."

At the Cron home, Pat was just sitting down to dinner.

When I mentioned the hotel, she jumped up, grabbed her coat, and we were on our way to Jennie Mae's.

"Watch me," Pat said. "This is how you run." She grabbed my hand and we ran all the way to the Stevensons' farm.

"Hey, you're not as slow as you used to be," she said.

"You run away from home and travel to Rye, New York, alone and see how much weight you lose!"

Pat told Jennie Mae about my athletic accomplishment. She took my other hand and the three of us seemed to fly down Victoria Street. I actually enjoyed moving fast enough to feel the wind on my face.

Back at the hotel, Aunt Rose had put out sandwiches, cookies, tarts, and tea. Pat and Jennie Mae filled their plates and I put a few items on mine, but I was too excited to eat. When we sat down at our own table, Nana told Billy and Llew they could join us.

The next three hours passed quietly. Mom and Nana knitted, the men played cards, and Aunt Rose puttered in the kitchen. Jennie Mae, Pat, and I worked on a 5,000-piece jigsaw puzzle, and Llew played cards, and later checkers, with Billy.

At eleven o'clock, Mr. Gibson ran in with a telegram. A ship confirmed hearing a plane flying low at 10:47 P.M. We all jumped up and cheered.

"But it was too foggy and rainy to confirm it visually," Mr. Gibson added.

Everyone sat down and turned to Bernt and Ed.

"It's probably just an isolated squall," Ed said.

"The weather office said her route would keep her away from the rain," Bernt reminded us.

Everyone went back to their activities except Nana, who had fallen asleep in her chair. Her head kept falling forward, and so Mom decided to take her into the bedroom off the kitchen. In better times, young girls working for Aunt Rose slept there. Billy tried to object to joining them, but his eyelids drooped and he couldn't focus well enough to argue.

Bernt and Ed asked to be wakened at 4:00 A.M., unless another message came in. They said good night and walked up to their rooms. Uncle Harry and Aunt Rose decided to stretch out for a few hours in their own rooms. Dad and Llew left because they had work to do at the store in the morning. Jennie Mae, Pat, and I crossed our arms on the table and dozed off.

I seemed to rise from a heavy fog into a roaring sound that filled my whole head. I saw eyes through a windshield, surrounded by water, ice, and flames. Then I dropped through the air.

I sat up suddenly. The noise and fog were gone. I was back in Aunt Rose's dining room.

I clasped my hands and looked up.

"Please don't let her die, God. Please," I prayed.

A hand on my shoulder made me jump. Uncle Harry whispered in my ear, "It's four in the morning."

He smiled at me and put his pocket watch back. I made a

deal with him: if he would wake Bernt and Ed, I would make the tea. He called me an angel and headed to the stairs.

While the four of us sipped our tea, the others slowly wakened and joined us. No one talked much until Aunt Rose came down. We told her there had been no news.

"No news is good news," she said. "I don't want to see those long faces. We need positive energy going out to our girl!"

"A little prayer wouldn't hurt," Nana said. She clasped her hands and we closed our eyes. "Dear God, watch over Amelia and take her safely to solid ground." She stopped and kept her head bowed so we could add our own words.

I imagined I was standing behind Amelia.

"You can do it," I told her. "I know you can think your way through any problem." I crossed my fingers and whispered, "Amen."

CHAPTER THIRTY-NINE

NEWS AT LAST

M ISS RORKE, OUR teacher, arrived and Uncle Harry rushed
into the kitchen to get her a cup of tea. They sat chatting,
and Uncle Harry seemed to be smiling a lot. When she was
finished, she asked me to bring any news to the school.

We drank endless cups of tea as the sun rose, and the
morning crept toward noon. There was little conversation
and less activity. Even Aunt Rose couldn't dispel the gloom
that had settled like a black cloak over all of us. She retreated
to the kitchen, where Mom joined her. Billy held a skein
of wool around both his hands while Nana rolled it into a
ball to continue her knitting. Pat and Jennie Mae played Xs
and Os, hangman, and checkers. I tried reading, I tried the
jigsaw puzzle, but nothing could distract me. The dream I
had last night kept haunting me.

At 11:45 A.M., the outside door burst open and those who
were sitting jumped to their feet. Mr. Gibson rushed in
waving a telegram. He couldn't seem to catch his breath, so

Uncle Harry grabbed the message. "She landed!" he shouted. "In a farmer's field, in Ireland. She's safe, she's safe!"

Mr. Gibson wiped his face with his handkerchief, smiling and nodding. We cheered and ran around hugging each other. Mr. Balchen had tears in his eyes and Mr. Gorski kept repeating over and over, "I knew she could do it. I knew she could do it."

I looked over at Mom. She stayed seated and gazed out the window beside the table. Before I could move toward her, Pat and Jennie Mae grabbed my hands. "Come on. We have to let Miss Rorke know Amelia landed safely."

We ran to the front door and almost flew up Victoria Street and along Harvey Street to the school. When Louise Crane opened the classroom door, we shouted, "She landed!" Everyone whooped and ran toward us. We hugged and patted each other's backs.

I could barely see Miss Rorke at the front of the class, and so I moved in her direction.

"What is Amelia like?" Oliver Watts asked me.

Before I could answer, someone else grabbed my arm. "Are you going to be a pilot like Amelia Earhart, Ginny?"

Without a moment's hesitation, I answered. "Yes, I am."

The words flew around the classroom: "Ginny's going to be a pilot like Amelia Earhart!" After some time had passed, Miss Rorke clapped her hands and the class fell silent. "Time to return to our school work," she said.

This was my cue to leave for the hotel. I waved goodbye

to everyone and slowly closed the door behind me. I wished with all my heart that I could stay, but school wasn't part of my life now.

I walked along Harvey Street to the corner of Victoria, but instead of continuing toward the hotel, I walked uphill to a boulder next to the railroad track. I climbed up onto its warmth and felt the sun on my back. I should have been the happiest girl in the world, but there was a tightness in my chest. My eyes filled with tears and I swiped them away.

"What's wrong with you, Ginny Ross?" I whispered. "Everything you've dreamed of is about to come true. You just have to reach out and take whatever Amelia offers."

I closed my eyes and saw Mom sitting alone at the hotel. She was the only one who wasn't jumping for joy. But why should that bother me? I could take flying lessons whether she liked it or not. I climbed off the rock and headed home. The sooner I told her how I felt, the better.

When I approached the store, Llew was opening crates out front. He ran to meet me, grabbed both my hands, and swung me around. "She did it!"

I smiled back at him. "Yes, she did."

"You don't seem excited."

"I've already cheered in the hotel, ran to the school and whooped it up with the class, but now I have to talk to Mom."

"She's in the store alone," he said. "Look. Your dad found some unopened crates in one of the sheds out back. He's like a kid at Christmas." Llew lifted the lid on one of them and showed me the hard bread stacked inside. "We're putting some of them out here to show people we have more to trade for what you need."

"That's great." I smiled again and squeezed his hand.

He opened the front door for me. "Good luck," he whispered.

Mom was standing behind the long counter, taking chocolates from a fancy box and putting them in an empty candy jar. "If people can't buy a whole box, maybe they'll ask for one or two."

"That's a good idea," I replied.

She opened another box and continued to fill the jar.

"I guess you heard Amelia landed safely," I continued.

"If you're here to talk about being a pilot, save your breath!" She looked up with anger blazing in her eyes.

"I've done everything to prove I'm capable of becoming a pilot. You're the only one who doesn't believe in me."

"I believe flying is for men."

"Amelia just flew across the Atlantic Ocean—alone!"

"She's the exception—and as I've said before, you are no Amelia Earhart."

"And as I've said before, I don't need to be tall, slim, and beautiful. I'm brave, determined, and smart!" I leaned over the counter to emphasize my point.

"Don't you raise your voice to me, young lady!" She waved her finger under my nose.

If she thought yelling and threatening were going to shut me up, she had another think coming. But I stepped back out of her reach, just to be on the safe side. She continued to fill the jar but didn't say another word. I hoped she realized the silent treatment wouldn't work, either. If I didn't solve this problem now, I would never be able to live my own life.

I sighed and started again. "I know I'm not the kind of daughter you want."

"Why on earth would you say such a thing?"

"I'm not pretty and graceful. I'm not talented like you. I can't play tennis or dance or sew or paint or play the piano or sing. But I can be a good pilot. Then I won't be an embarrassment to you."

Mom's hands stopped moving and she kept her eyes down. "You're not an embarrassment to me. But furthermore, there's no money for flying lessons."

"I have time to work for Aunt Rose. Amelia says I can delay school and my flying lessons until the time is right."

"You know what happened the last time you left home."

"But our lives are different now," I said. "Dad says he and Llew want to run the store. They found a few more supplies out back. You can trade them for what you need."

She didn't answer.

I couldn't think of anything else to say, so I waited for her next objection.

She looked up with tears running down her face. "I don't want to lose you."

"I'll be making money while I'm flying, and sending it home. You won't lose my help."

She reached across the counter and took both my hands in hers. "I don't want to lose *you*."

My eyes filled up with tears. I never thought she cared about me, let alone.... The words got caught in my throat, but I needed to know the answer.

"You love me?" I whispered.

"Of course I love you," she said. She looked down at our hands again. "I just don't show it the way I should."

The lump in my throat was so big I could barely breathe.

She smiled and said, "I must admit, I realized there was more to you when you ran away and we all fell apart."

"But you followed me in my dreams."

She laughed. "I suppose we are an unforgettable bunch."

Just then Dad walked in. "I think we're temporarily back in business, ladies. The new supplies won't last long, but we'll face each day as it comes."

SEPTEMBER 1932

———◦‣———

FACING EACH DAY as it comes is what we've done. Dad stands in the doorway of the store, with a long apron tied under his suit coat, and greets people as they walk by. They're still not buying much, but they stop in to socialize. They join Nana, who sits beside the stove knitting, while Mom lays out her patterns on the short counter. She sews for the ladies in St. John's who can afford new clothes. In the evenings Dad stays home and we listen to the radio, play cards, or read.

Papa's goodwill hasn't been forgotten. All those who received groceries from him, even when they couldn't pay, still bring in rabbits, fish, seal meat, and vegetables when they have some to share. "Put it against my bill, Mr. Ross," they say.

Llew has convinced Billy he isn't too young to learn the business. He sweeps the floor and helps with the deliveries. He's looking right proud of himself these days.

"Llew did these jobs when he was ten years old, but I'm only seven!" Billy says.

Jennie Mae and I still meet Pat in front of her house every weekday morning. When we get to Harvey Street, they walk to school and I walk to the hotel. A few days earlier, Pat showed us a report she wrote about meeting Amelia Earhart. She took it to Mr. Butt at the *Harbour Grace Standard,* and he published it. She is well on her way to becoming a "famous" reporter.

Miss Rorke comes to the hotel three evenings a week to tutor me. I finished grade eight by the end of June, and I've been working on grade nine since then. She said I should be finished grade nine by January. Then I would just have grade ten and grade eleven left. I'll be finished school in no time, even before Pat and Jennie Mae.

As soon as my lesson is finished, Uncle Harry comes into the kitchen to make Miss Rorke and me tea. He sits at the table with us and we chat. I've never seen him smile and blush so much in my whole life.

Elizabeth Harris and I exchange letters regularly. She tells me what she, Edwina, Ann, and Maude are doing. Sometimes they add a P.S. to Elizabeth's letters. I'm happy to tell her that Mom's lecturing and hitting have stopped. I think these last four months are the happiest I've ever seen Mom. Elizabeth is relieved that our lives have changed for the better.

As for Amelia and me, her letter arrived about three months after her flight. Following her awards, medals, and ticker-tape parade, she had many speaking engagements to fulfill.

She and Mr. Putnam continue to search for ways they can involve more women in aviation. Of course, Amelia's recent flight will be a great help, but they'd still like to find a school to partner with. Recently they heard that Purdue University in Indiana has had its own airport for two years now. They're excited by this news, but they don't know if a partnership is possible. Amelia is going to keep me posted on any developments.

I read the letter and then hand it to Mom. After she reads it, she sits in Papa's chair by the stove and smiles up at me.

"Maybe you will make us all proud some day."

GLOSSARY

---◄◦►---

barnstormer: the name given to pilots who made money by taking people for short flights. They often used farmers' fields to take off and land. Many were pilots from the First World War.
"I remember when I was in Boston and a barnstormer took me up in his plane for a two-dollar ride." (page 193)

Bowring Brothers: a company that supplied merchants with the products they sold in their stores.
"The next shipment of supplies from Bowring Brothers arrives tomorrow." (page 24)

brewis: a common Newfoundland meal made of salt cod and hard bread or hardtack. Pronounced like "bruise."
"What I really wanted was fish, brewis, and lassy toast." (page 36)

chenille: a thick, soft cotton, often with nubs or bumps on it.
"With the chenille bedspread I made a knot around the leg of the large oak bed." (page 152)

dandy: someone who is smart in dress and manners.
"Joey kissed our hands and the fishermen called him a right dandy." (page 133)

doff: an action, meaning to take something off as a sign of respect.
"The fishermen doffed their caps to Elizabeth and me as they took our hands." (page 133)

dory: a boat with a flat bottom and high sides used for fishing.
"And there was Llew on our wharf passing supplies down to a fisherman in dory." (page 73)

exhaust port: the opening that allows the escape of used gas or vapour from an engine.
"The plane coughed and sputtered in the cold and puffs of smoke escaped the exhaust port." (page 20)

fuselage: the central body portion of a plane used for the pilot, crew, passengers, or cargo.
"I reached up and placed my hands on the fuselage." (page 9)

grate: a metal frame used to cover an opening. In old houses there were square openings between floors to allow the heat from one floor to rise to the floor above.
"I hurried to the grate in the floor next to my bedside table." (page 75)

hard bread: (sometimes called hardtack) a thick, oval-shaped biscuit. It must be soaked in water to soften before it is boiled or fried and served.
"I walked to the long counter where he was opening a box of hard bread." (page 59)

"I'se the B'y": a well-known Newfoundland folk song, meaning "I'm the boy."
"I heard faint accordion music and a chorus of 'I'se the B'y.'" (page 128)

lassy toast: toast spread with butter and molasses.
"What I really wanted was fish, brewis, and lassy toast." (page 36)

molasses: thick syrup made from raw sugar. It is a dark brown colour.
"You're as slow as molasses in January." (page 7)

mummers: at Christmastime, people in Newfoundland traditionally go from house to house in costumes, with their faces covered. They are given something to eat and drink in return for their entertainment. The people in the house have to guess who they are.
"The mummers sang and all our neighbours joined in." (page 128)

port stabilizer: the horizontal part of the tail on a plane. The port stabilizer is on the left (port) side.
"This slightly damaged the plywood covering the port stabilizer." (page 180)

pound: what paper money was called in Newfoundland in 1932. It can be worth various amounts: one, five, ten, or more. In 1931–32, when this story takes place, Newfoundland was not part of Canada and England was Newfoundland's home country, so they used British currency.
"Elizabeth offered me five pounds for the trip to Boston." (page 131)

right: very.
"She thought she was right special." (page 6)

running board: the footboard on either side of a vehicle. It is used to step up into the vehicle.
"Uncle Harry stood on the running board of Mike Hayes's taxi with Aunt Rose's megaphone up to his mouth." (page 189)

salt cod: a codfish that has had its head and tail cut off. It is split down the belly, cleaned, covered with salt, and laid flat in the sun to dry.
"Sea air and the smell of salt cod filled the room." (page 37)

some: very or a lot.

"It had been some exciting when the plane landed yesterday afternoon." (page 8)

struts: those parts of the plane that support or brace the wings.

"We stopped in the shadow of the wing and listened to the wind whistling in the struts." (page 9)

throttle: the instrument in a plane that is used to increase or decrease the speed.

"I started the engine and pushed the throttle forward." (page 13)

winter vegetables: root vegetables such as potatoes, carrots, turnips, and parsnips. They are stored in the winter in root cellars to keep them from drying out.

"We finished our baked cod and winter vegetables and returned to our seats." (page 131)

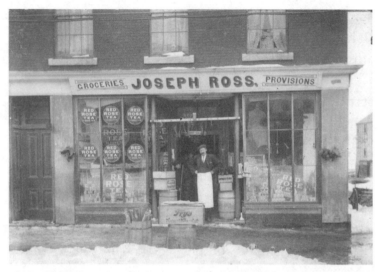

The real-life Papa's store, with Papa standing in the doorway.

The Ross family home was on the second and third storeys above the store.

L–R: Ginny, her dad, her mom, and her brother Billy.

Harbour Grace airstrip with Lady Lake on the right. The bay is on the left but can't be seen in this photograph.

The City of New York when it landed in Harbour Grace.

The Archibald Boot and Shoe Factory, where Ginny's uncle Harry worked until it closed.

Rose (L) and her brother Harry standing in front of the wing section of The City of New York. Note that Rose is wearing shorts; she was ahead of her time!

Munn's premises at Point O' Beach.

A view of Harbour Grace from above the railroad track. The large building on the bottom right is the school.

Llewellyn Crane with Daisy pulling Papa's grocery cart.

Water Street in downtown Harbour Grace. The men on the left are standing in front of the telegraph office.

Mom and Pop Davis on their wedding day.

Billy and Ginny.

Henry Mears holding his dog, Tailwind.

Bernt Balchen and Ed Gorski refuelling Amelia's plane.

Uncle Harry (middle) in his role as airport supervisor.

Amelia Earhart stepping out of Mike Hayes's taxi. She is holding the Thermos of soup the real life Ginny Ross made for her.

Amelia Earhart talking to reporters after she landed in Harbour Grace.

PHOTO CREDITS

———◦———

Page 226: All photos courtesy of the Ross family.

Page 227: Top photo courtesy of Library & Archives Canada, PA-127541. Bottom photo courtesy of The Rooms Provincial Archives, A46-121.

Page 228: Top photo courtesy of Library & Archives Canada, PA-201474. Bottom photo courtesy of the Archibald family.

Page 229: Top photo courtesy of the Archibald family. Bottom photo courtesy of Jennie Mae (Stevenson) Alley.

Page 230: Top photo courtesy of The Rooms Provincial Archives, A32-58. Bottom photo courtesy of Harbour Grace Tourism.

Page 231: Top photos courtesy of the Ross family. Bottom photo courtesy of the National Air and Space Museum, NASM-00141987.

Page 232: Top photo courtesy of The Rooms Provincial Archives, H5-35. Bottom photo courtesy of Library & Archives Canada, PA-127542.

Page 233: Top photo courtesy of Library & Archives Canada, PA-057855. Bottom photo courtesy of The Rooms Provincial Archives, H5-34.

AUTHOR'S NOTE

———◦———

I INTERVIEWED THE people who were still alive when I was writing the book in order to include their memories: Pat Cron, Jennie Mae Alley (Stevenson), Llewellyn Crane, Lilly Ryan (Shanahan), Marjorie Davis, Louise Crane (Archibald), and Hope and Lote Whitman. Although he doesn't appear in the book, Uncle Wool Archibald (Uncle Harry's nephew) supplied many true stories.

All of the information about the Mears and Brown flight is accurate except the date. The actual crash at the Harbour Grace Airfield took place in August of 1930. I changed the date to 1931 so that their flight would be closer in time to Amelia's. I also changed Henry Brown's name to George Brown to avoid confusion with Henry Mears.

The details about Amelia's flight are also accurate, including the soup Ginny made at her Aunt Rose's hotel for Amelia to take on her flight. There is a wonderful picture of Amelia holding the Thermos on page 233.

ACKNOWLEDGEMENTS

———◇———

I OWE THANKS to many people for assistance with this book. The following helped me in various ways:

Martha Attema (children's book author) first heard Ginny's story orally and insisted it could be a book.

Shannon Ryan (1941–2016) was a historian, retired from Memorial University of Newfoundland, who introduced me to Newfoundland history, to proper interviewing techniques, and to the women in his life—Margaret, his wife, and Lilly Shanahan Ryan, his mother. All three shared their lives with me.

Sandra Ronayne (Archivist, Still and Moving Pictures, The Rooms) introduced me to Harbour Grace in 1931–1932, through black-and-white photographs, and suddenly I was part of this community.

Charles and Joanne Archibald (Harbour Grace cousins) provided family photographs and local knowledge, both historical and current.

Ian Leslie (Canada Aviation and Space Museum) provided material in the form of books and magazine articles on the airplanes and technical practices of the 1930s.

Dr. Susan Adams and Nick Kelefas (pilots) helped me understand the technical aspects of airplanes and flying.

Amanda and Joseph Boyden (Creative Writing Program at the University of New Orleans) saw this book in its earliest stages and encouraged me to keep going.

Antanas Sileika, Marsha Skrypuch, Tim Wynne-Jones, and Richard Scrimger (The Humber School of Creative Writing and Performing Arts) guided me through the creative process.

Paul Butler (Wordpress) added the final polish.

The following people read and commented on the book as it evolved: Elizabeth Ashworth, Martha Attema, Suzanne Brooks, Helen Langford, Janet Zimbalatti and Roz Zimbalatti.

My family, Don, James, Jenn, Mike, Sue, Caleb, Maeve, Charlie, and Phaedra, have lived with this book as long as I have and provided their love and support.